Contents

Illustrated by **John Harrold**

Story colouring by **Gina Hart**

Original stories by **James Henderson**
and **Ian Robinson**

Adapted by **Vicky Reed**

Design and colour reproduction by **Scriveners**

This book belongs to:

. . . .

John Harrold

RUPERT

The EXPRESS NEWSPAPERS Annual

Published by Express Newspapers, The Northern & Shell Building, Number 10 Lower Thames Street, London EC3R 6EN. A Northern & Shell Media Company. Email: rupert.bear@express.co.uk
© Express Newspapers 2005. Rupert characters TM and © Express Newspapers, 2005.

No. 70

£7.50

RUPERT

Nutwood Common is looking its best,
Fresh, green and sparkling – full of zest.

Nutwood Common is looking its best this morning, all fresh, green and sparkling. As Rupert skirts the woods, the bird-song is about as loud as he's ever heard it. Then suddenly, louder than the birds, come squeaks of alarm and the thud of running feet. Rupert turns towards the sounds and sees the Rabbit twins, Reggie and Rex, burst from the trees. The twins are pals of Rupert and he knows that it doesn't take much to frighten them. But now they look very scared indeed as they flee from the woods.

and the Speaking Pool

The Rabbit twins burst from the trees,
They both look scared, Rupert sees.

Speechless, Rex clutches Rupert's arm,
The brothers now must raise the alarm.

No doubt about it, the Rabbit twins are scared stiff. Rex clutches Rupert's arm, speechless with fear, while Reggie can only point back at the woods they have just fled and stammer, "A v-v-v ..." At last Rupert has to speak firmly, "Come on, the pair of you. Calm down and tell me what's up." It's Rex who manages to speak first. "A v-voice!" he squeaks. "Oh, such a sad voice! Near the forest pool we heard it, didn't we Reggie? It sounded like someone in trouble. But oh, Rupert – there was no-one there!"

"We heard a sad voice, near the pool,"
"But no-one's there – I am no fool."

talks with the Rabbit twins

"A voice," says Rupert, "No-one there?"
"Sounds like a trick is in the air."

He sets off; he'll take his chances,
The twins turn tail, exchange scared glances.

Under foot the branches crunch,
But Rupert has a nervous hunch.

Now near the pool he hears a 'pop!'
A voice begins, it doesn't stop.

"A voice?" Rupert echoes. "No-one there?" The twins gulp and nod. "Someone must have been playing a trick," Rupert says. "There was no one!" cries Rex. "The voice came from – oh, you won't believe us!" "Believe what?" Rupert asks. The twins exchange glances. "No, you'll say we're being silly," mutters Reggie, and the pair refuse to say any more. "I know, let's all go to the pool and make a search," Rupert says. "Not likely!" the horrified twins chorus and turn tail. So Rupert ventures into the woods alone.

Rupert likes these woods. He and his pals often play in them. And today they look no different from usual. Sunbeams strike down between the branches and last year's leaves crunch under foot. Somehow, though, Rupert feels, well, just a bit nervous. "You're as bad as Reggie and Rex," he tells himself sternly, and on he pushes to the heart of the woods and the pool. It is quiet. Within sight of the pool he halts. Silence. Not a thing stirs. Then – a pop! And a voice groans, "This is awful!"

RUPERT
hears a voice

The groaning voice makes Rupert jump,
He searches while his heart does thump.

Never feeling more alone,
He turns to go but hears a moan.

He is quite brave, but now he feels
Rather scared, and takes to his heels.

Those Rabbit twins were quite right,
The voice has given him a fright.

Rupert has almost jumped out of his skin at that sudden pop and the groaning voice. But then he thinks, "I can't run away. Maybe someone's been hurt. I must look." So, a bit shakily, he calls, "I say, who's there?" No answer. He tries again. Silence. "I'd better search round the pool," he mutters. So he starts off, looking behind trees, peering into bushes and every now and then calling, "Who's there?" and "Where are you?" No reply. At last he turns to go and – pop! Followed by a moan, "Oh, dear!"

That does it! He has seen for himself that there's no-one near the pool. Yet, once again – that voice! For a little bear Rupert is usually pretty brave. But suddenly the pool and the woods he has known so long and likes so much, have become frightening. He takes to his heels. No wonder the Rabbit twins were scared, he thinks. At any time it doesn't take much to frighten them. And no wonder they were horrified at the idea of returning to the pool. Now all he wants is to get well away from it.

9

RUPERT

meets the old Professor

Down the path, pursued by fears,
Something heavy Rupert hears.

Peeping out from his hiding place,
He's glad to see a friendly face.

Professor smiles when he sees
It's Rupert dashing from the trees.

He heard the Rabbits' tale of woe
After Rupert he had to go.

The path Rupert is fleeing along is narrow and in places so overgrown it almost disappears in the bushes. And it is in just such a place that Rupert is brought to a stop by something he hears. Something – large and heavy by the sound of it – is pushing through the bushes towards him. In a flash he has left the path and dodged behind a big tree. He holds his breath and watches. Whatever is coming is almost here. The bushes across the path part ... Whew! It's his friend the old Professor!

"Professor!" The old man jumps at the sudden cry. But his face breaks into a smile when he sees who dashes out from behind a tree. "Rupert!" He exclaims. "I was looking for you. I was driving near the woods and I met with the Rabbit twins, very frightened. They gabbled about 'something awful' in the woods and said you'd gone alone to investigate. So I thought I ought to check. But it looks as if they were talking nonsense." Rupert shakes his head. "No," he says. "They weren't talking nonsense."

RUPERT
and the Professor investigate

The Professor just cannot believe,
But Rupert says he would not deceive.

"If there's a voice it must belong ..."
"Let us go back and see what's wrong."

Silly stories they plan to stop,
But at the pool they hear a 'pop!'

A bubble rises, the voice says ...
"Oh dear," – the two pals stand and gaze.

The Professor stares at Rupert. "Surely you don't believe that the Rabbits heard some voice or other and that no-one was there?" he exclaims. "I didn't at first," says Rupert, "But I went to investigate and heard it too. It sort of moaned. I searched all around the pool. No-one was there!" "Poppycock!" cries the other. "If there's a voice it belongs to someone. If you can't see that someone then it's because he's out of sight somewhere. So let's have no scary nonsense. We're going back to look. Come on!"

Nothing would have tempted Rupert back to the forest pool on his own. Even with the Professor holding his hand he isn't terribly keen on the idea. But back they go, the Professor vowing that he's going to "nip silly scare stories in the bud". He stops, though, when, as they reach the pool, there is a pop and a groan, "What shall I do?" As the pair stare at the water a bubble surfaces. It pops and the voice moans, "Oh dear! Oh dear!" The Professor gasps. "The-the voice came from the bubble!" he whispers.

11

RUPERT

goes diving

"Someone must be in deep trouble,"
"We shall help them at the double."

A diving suit will let them go,
Into the pool, see what's below.

His fear now is no longer on show,
About the voice he wants to know.

The Professor's house is quite near,
Soon he returns with diving gear.

The Professor sinks to his knees and peers into the pool, then turns to Rupert and says, "Plainly someone or something in the pool is in trouble. We must do what we can to help." "But what?" Rupert asks. "Well," says the Professor, "I'd send my little assistant down to look – you know I designed a diving suit for him. But he's in bed with a bad cold, so I thought ..." "That I might go," Rupert breaks in. "Right! I'll have a go." The Professor beams: "I'll fetch the suit. Wait here." And off he goes.

Thanks to the Professor Rupert isn't frightened about the mysterious voice any more - just curious. He lies on the bank, peering at the water, waiting for the bubbles to rise, pop and release a moan about how awful it is in the pool. The Professor's right," thinks Rupert. There is someone or something down there in trouble. I just hope I can help." In no time at all, the Professor is back with the diving gear. He'd left his car near the woods and his tower home is quite near. "Ready, Rupert?" he cries.

RUPERT

looks around underwater

Although the suit is not a perfect fit,
Rupert makes the best of the diving kit.

"Go down and take a look around,"
"I'll pull you out, see what you found."

This pool is dark and very deep,
The lamp switched on, he must keep.

The mystery came from down here,
An answer will very soon be quite clear.

The Professor's assistant is not quite as small as Rupert so a couple of adjustments have to be made to his diving suit for it to fit. It has a special breathing pack and a valve that allows Rupert to hear and be heard. There is a lamp to go with it. The Professor fixes a safety line to the suit and tells Rupert: "Go down and take a quick look around for the owner of the voice but don't wander about. Then tug the line and I'll bring you up." "Right, here goes!" Rupert says and jumps into the pool.

The pool is not very big but it is quite a bit deeper than Rupert expected. It is also dark, and almost at once he has to switch on the underwater lamp. He keeps the beam pointing down so that he will see the bed of the pool in good time. As he goes down he thinks about the voice that came from the bursting bubbles and tells himself, "It's true someone must have spoken but can they really be down here? Well, maybe we'll see very shortly." And a few moments later, standing on the bottom, he does see.

A barrel is caught right in his beam,
Bubbles rising, what can it mean?

A pair of hands wave frantically,
Who is inside, he now can see!

His pal Bingo, the clever pup,
Is trapped in there, but what is up?

Bingo's words are caught in a bubble,
To the rear is where there's trouble.

Just ahead of him and caught in the beam of his lamp, Rupert can make out what at first looks like a large barrel on its side. But the end of it is made of glass and on top is a sort of tube from which bubbles are rising. Behind the glass something is moving. Rupert can see a pair of hands waving. Whoever they belong to is plainly frightened rather than being frightening. Cautiously Rupert advances on the barrel-like thing, his lamp beam trained on it. Suddenly, he sees whose hands they are. "Bingo!" he gasps.

Seated at a wheel behind the glass is Rupert's pal Bingo, the clever pup. "What on earth's happening?" Rupert cries. But he can't hear a word of Bingo's reply – if it is a reply. As he speaks, though, bubbles emerge from the tube above him and disappear upwards. And suddenly Rupert sees! Somehow his pal's words are being trapped in the bubbles and carried to the surface. Now Bingo points to the rear of his strange craft as if wanting Rupert to look. Plainly something is wrong there so goes back to look.

14

RUPERT

meets a frog

What Rupert sees leaves him agog,
The craft is held by a huge frog!

Too well he plainly cannot see,
A tadpole he thinks this to be.

The observation is quite daft,
Who could so mistake this odd craft?

"It's not a tadpole," Rupert says,
But Frog makes sure here it stays.

Rupert examines Bingo's strange craft as he goes to see what's wrong at the back. "It's a bit like a tadpole," he thinks when he sees a tail at the rear of the bulky body. Then he gasps when he sees what is clutching the end of a tail – a bespectacled frog. "Who is that?" it demands peering short-sightedly. So Rupert says who he is and asks politely, "What are you doing?" The frog replies, "As the Frog King's Chief Steward I am holding this awful giant tadpole while I decide what to do about it."

"You see," says the frog, "if this tadpole grew into a frog it would be bigger than our King and that would never do." Now, it's true Rupert himself thought Bingo's craft looked a bit like a tadpole, but only a bit. The frog must be awfully short-sighted to take it for a real one. "It's not a tadpole," Rupert says. "It's a sort of submarine and my chum's in it. Come and see." The frog looks doubtful. Still, it nods agreement. But before joining Rupert it wedges the craft's tail between some rocks.

Bingo and Frog look on with surprise,
Frog must do something for his eyes.

He agrees to let the craft go,
The way to the surface he will show.

"I hope your friend is not too cross,"
Says Frog, who is now at a loss.

"I'm sure that he will understand,"
Says Rupert as Frog lends a hand.

It's hard to say who's the more surprised when Bingo and the frog come face-to-face. "Oh, dear," the frog says. "There is someone in there. Even I can see that now. You know, I thought it didn't feel like a tadpole – even a giant one. I must do something about these specs of mine." And the frog looks as embarrassed as a frog can. "Then, please, will you let go now?" Rupert asks. "I'll do better than that," the frog declares. "I shall take both of you back to the surface – fast. It's the least I can do."

After letting Bingo know by signs what's happening, Rupert returns to the tail of the craft where the frog is busy removing the rocks that were holding it. "I hope your friend isn't too cross," the frog says. "I was only doing my duty as the Frog King's Chief Steward. The trouble is I'm so short-sighted." Rupert says he's sure Bingo will understand. "Good," says the frog. "Now hop on my back." And as soon as Rupert is in place it grasps the tail of Bingo's craft and launches itself towards the surface.

RUPERT

and his pal climb ashore

The Professor is so very surprised,
At what appears before his eyes.

"Help us to shore," is Rupert's call,
"And then I shall explain it all."

Bingo recounts his tale of woe,
His craft was held by unseen foe.

The frog, so sorry for his plight,
Dives in the water out of sight.

The Professor's eyes pop when Bingo's craft breaks the surface of the pool and he sees who's in it. He has heard Bingo's words carried up by the bubbles but he has not recognised the voice. And he gasps when a second later Rupert appears too, seemingly having come up by himself. Then his mouth drops open in astonishment when Rupert rises further out of the water and the old man finds himself looking into the short-sighted eyes of a very big frog. "Help us ashore," Rupert calls, "and I'll explain everything."

Excitedly Rupert and Bingo pour out their story as they are helped ashore. Bingo tells of trying out the underwater craft he'd built and suddenly finding it held tight by something unseen. Then Rupert tells how the short-sighted frog mistook the craft for a sort of giant tadpole. "How odd!" cries Bingo. "I call it 'The Tadpole' because it's propelled and steered by its tail like a real one." At this the frog smiles. But it says, "I'd still better see about new specs – goodbye!" and it dives out of sight.

17

Bingo's tickled by his troubles,
And how his plea rose by up bubbles.

"If we can create it," he says with a laugh,
"We can call it the Bubblegraph!"

Adventure over – time to go,
What next is what they want to know?

Will the Professor really try,
To make bubbles in which words fly?

Bingo can't get over his Tadpole being taken for a real one. "Shows how good it is," he chuckles. Rupert says he still can't understand how Bingo's words were carried to the surface in bubbles. "It shouldn't happen," the Professor says. "But it did. Possibly it has to do with that breather tube on top of the Tadpole. We must investigate later." This appeals to Bingo. "If we can make it happen," he cries, "We'll call it the Bubblegraph for sending underwater messages!" "It's a big 'if'," laughs the Professor.

The adventure is over for now. Rupert gets out of his diving suit and Bingo moors The Tadpole to be collected later. As the three friends leave the forest pool, Rupert asks the Professor: "Are you really going to try and make a thing for carrying words in bubbles?" "Oh, I think we must try," the Professor says. "Though I'm not sure what use it would be. I might also start thinking about better glasses for short-sighted frogs!"

THE END

Guess the Story

As you read through Rupert's adventures, can you guess which story each picture comes from?

When you have finished reading the annual and filled in this page check your answers on page 109.

_____ _____ _____ _____

_____ _____ _____ _____

_____ _____ _____ _____

_____ _____ _____ _____

RUPERT

*After school on one fine spring day
Ottoline asks Rupert home to play.*

One spring afternoon, when school has finished, Ottoline asks Rupert if he would like to come back to her house for tea. "Yes, please!" he says. Rupert always likes visiting Nutwood Manor, Ottoline's house, because the Manor has so many rooms to explore. "Have you found any more secret passages?" he asks. "No," says Ottoline. "But there is something I want to show you. It's a mystery! We're nearly there now, so you won't have long to wait ..."

and the Wind Chimes

Nutwood Manor is her home,
Many rooms to explore and roam.

On the steps Rupert hears a noise,
A tinkling sound, it's not like toys.

"See if you can tell what's new?" says Ottoline as they reach the house. Rupert steps inside and starts to look for clues. Almost at once, he hears a high, tinkling sound coming from upstairs. "Wh... what's that?" he blinks. "The mystery I have brought you to see!" says Ottoline. "Can you guess what it is yet?" "No," says Rupert. "It sounds like lots of little bells ringing in the distance ..." "Nearly right," says Ottoline. "Come and see, they are hanging in my room."

"The mystery I've brought you to see,"
Says Ottoline, "Has been foxing me!"

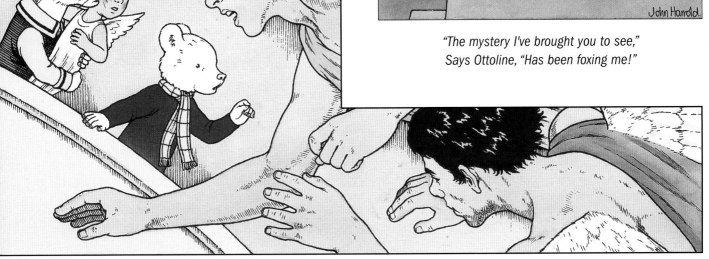

Wind chimes jangle, they make a din
The window's closed, no air gets in.

From where the draught comes no-one knows,
Behind the boxes full of clothes?

Around the boxes Rupert peers,
A shadowy, baby figure appears.

A baby wind with wings and tail
Gets a fright and starts to wail.

"Wind chimes!" says Rupert. "Yes," says Ottoline "but there's something strange going on," she says pointing to the chimes jangling to and fro. Rupert shrugs. "But, look Rupert, the window is closed!" Rupert gasps realising that it is not the wind causing the chimes to stir and follows the source of the air to an array of boxes on the top of Ottoline's chest of drawers. "What ever it is, it is coming from there," points Rupert.

Rupert climbs on a chair to reach the top of the chest of drawers to investigate the draught and as he pushes the boxes aside a small shadowy figure appears. "He looks like a baby ghost!" exclaims Ottoline. With a cry of alarm, the baby flies past the chums and darts towards an open door. "Oh dear," says Ottoline. "I think you've given the poor thing rather a fright."

RUPERT

meets a baby wind

As Rupert calls, the baby glides
Into a cupboard where it hides.

"Don't be afraid," says Ottoline,
"With Rupert and I, you will be fine."

A chance to leave makes baby cry
And this makes Rupert wonder why?

The Weather Clerk will know what to do,
Into the skies we'll send a clue.

"Come back!" calls Rupert, but the baby disappears into an open cupboard. "I think he's trying to hide from us!" whispers Ottoline. "Perhaps he is shy of strangers ..." She kneels down and calls gently, "Don't be afraid. Rupert and I only want to help you. We've never seen a flying baby before and wondered where you came from? You can play with the wind chimes again if you like, or there are lots of other toys you can borrow instead ..."

"I think he must be a young wind who flew in through your window, perhaps we should let him fly out to find his parents?" says Rupert. The baby looks at the window and starts to cry. "Why does he not want to go?" asks Ottoline. They both want to help but are unsure what to do when Rupert cries, "I know, the Weather Clerk will know where all the winds come from. Let me take your kite to send a message to him."

RUPERT

finds the Weather Clerk

From a cupboard comes Ottoline's kite,
On it there's a message to write.

Off to the common, they will try
To fly the kite high in the sky.

But there's no wind, the kite lies flat.
Surely the wind can help with that?

Go baby wind and start to blow,
Above the clouds the kite will go.

"I will write a message to the Weather Clerk on this kite," says Rupert smiling. "If we fly it high enough the Clerk will find it and come and help. He will see the kite from his Weather Station." "Let's try the common," says Rupert. "Bill and I often go there to fly our kite." So, Rupert, Ottoline and the baby wind make their way across the common to find a perfect place to fly the kite.

Ottoline is dismayed there is no breeze to make the kite fly. "I know," says Rupert, "We are forgetting our little friend, I'm sure he knows how to fly kites!" Holding the kite up he urges the baby to blow, while Ottoline holds the string firmly. The kite and the baby disappear off high into the clouds. "I hope he is alright up there alone," says Ottoline. "He won't be able to see us from that height."

RUPERT

flies in the cloud-hopper

From the clouds a ladder does drop.
The pair climb up, where will it stop?

The Weather Clerk is waiting there,
His cloud-hopper is as light as air.

Above the clouds the 'Hopper' speeds,
The Weather Clerk explains his needs.

"I'm glad you're here, I need to learn,"
"Zeph's parents are causing me concern."

Suddenly the kite falls to the ground and a ladder appears from between the clouds. "Look, a rope-ladder!" exclaims Ottoline. "As soon as we can reach the ladder we can climb up and see what the Clerk says ..." As they emerge above the clouds they find the Weather Clerk sitting in a strange looking plane. "It's called the cloud-hopper," he announces. "I use it for journeys all around the globe. I am so glad you found Zeph, but I need your help with a bigger mystery. It is something that threatens the whole weather system. Climb aboard both of you."

As soon as everyone is safely aboard they speed off to the Weather Station with Zeph the baby wind flying above. "I knew it was Zeph the moment I saw him through my telescope. He often comes to see me with his mother, the South Wind," says the Clerk. Rupert explains how they found Zeph in Nutwood, and that they thought he may be able to help. "You were quite right to send me a note," explains the Clerk, "But I am very worried about Zeph's parents."

RUPERT
arrives at the Weather Station

All the Winds are Zeph's relation
But not been seen at the Weather Station.

Clouds are still, no wind in the sky
But still he has no answer why!

Zeph points ahead, he wants to go home
But he can't find the way alone.

His home is very far away,
"We can take him," the two friends say.

Inside the Weather Station, the Clerk explains how Zeph's parents are the North and South Winds and his uncles are the East and West Winds, and points to a wind chart. "But why have they left Zeph alone?" puzzles Ottoline. "I don't know," says the Clerk frowning. "I have not seen the winds since yesterday morning. The skies calmed and the clouds stopped moving. I really am very worried. They have never let me down before."

Zeph reaches out towards the picture on the chart. "Look, he wants to go home!" cries Ottoline. "The four winds live in a remote tower on the Equator, but I dare not leave the Weather Station for more than a few moments," says the Clerk. "Let us go!" says Ottoline. "We can take Zeph with us." "Excellent," smiles the Clerk. "Take the cloud-hopper, a map and my compass to show you the way and then just keep flying due south."

The cloud-hopper will get them there
And Zeph will be able to guide the bear.

Now off into the sky they zoom,
They'll steer around if storm clouds loom!

Below them Nutwood's a tiny dot
While the sun is getting extremely hot.

In the distance far across the sea,
"A tower," Rupert cries with glee.

Leading the way to the cloud-hopper, the Weather Clerk tells Rupert and Ottoline that Zeph will follow behind. "He is too young to fly alone, but he should be able to recognise the tower and guide you when you get near ..." The chums climb aboard, with Rupert at the controls. "Quite simple, really!" smiles the Clerk. "Ottoline can keep an eye on the compass, while you just follow her directions. You shouldn't meet any storm clouds, but try to steer round them if you do!"

The cloud-hopper flies on quietly over Nutwood until they reach the coast. "Keep going!" calls Ottoline. "The compass points straight out to sea." "What fun," laughs Rupert. "I wonder how we'll recognise the equator?" After flying over an expanse of ocean they finally see an island, but no sign of a tower. "I think I see ..." she begins, but Rupert cuts her off with a sudden cry. "That must be it, straight ahead. It looks just like a lighthouse!"

RUPERT

lands at the tower

On the top a weather vane sits,
Excitedly ahead Zeph flits.

The chums draw close, look where to land,
By now they are a cheerful band.

They look for a spot to land on the floor,
Zeph rushes forward towards the door.

A spiral staircase winds around.
They follow until they reach the ground.

As the chums get closer to the island, they see the tower has a weather vane on top, with a spinning figure that points the way. Zeph gives an excited cry and flits on ahead. "He's showing us where to land," says Ottoline. Rupert steers the cloud-hopper to a flat ledge on the roof of the tower. "There's just enough room," he calls. "It's like the Professor's tower in Nutwood. Bodkin climbs up on the roof to use the flag pole." "There's the door!" cries Ottoline. "There must be a staircase down ..."

Climbing out of the cloud-hopper, Rupert and Ottoline follow Zeph to the door. The baby wind pushes against it but is too small to manage on his own. Rupert turns the handle and starts to push too. The heavy door swings open, revealing a spiral staircase, which the pair begin to clamber down. "It is like a lighthouse!" says Ottoline. "We'll go round and round until we reach the bottom ..." Zeph seems delighted to be home and hurries on ahead of the chums, leading the way.

RUPERT

and friends search the tower

Through a curtain Zeph leads inside,
"We must find your mother," they cried.

Another room, varieties of shell,
No sign of mother, no clues to tell.

On the landing they hear a voice,
To go down the stairs is their next choice.

Zeph's parents talking, it must be!
Straight away they hurry to see.

The stairs lead down to a circular landing, where all the rooms have curtains rather than doors. "Can you show us the way to find your mother?" asks Ottoline. Zeph glides into a spacious room decorated with shells. "From the South Seas!" says Rupert. The baby wind searches for his mother, but the room is clearly empty. There's no one here!" blinks Ottoline. "Now what shall we do?"

Upset that his mother's room is empty, Zeph begins to cry. "There, there ..." says Ottoline. "I'm sure we'll find her soon." "Listen!" says Rupert. "I think I can hear someone ..." The chums go out to the landing and listen carefully. Sure enough, the sound of voices is coming from downstairs ... "It must be your parents," says Rupert. "I expect they're wondering where you can be." Hurrying down, he leads the way, while Ottoline and Zeph follow closely behind.

RUPERT

sees Billy Blizzard

Raised voices heard as they draw near,
So round the stairs Rupert does peer.

"It's Billy Blizzard!" he says with fear,
"Whatever is he doing here?"

Inching forward Rupert can see
Billy's plan is so dastardly.

Four Winds held – each in a gauze sack,
Billy was banished but now he's back.

As they near the foot of the stairs, Rupert stops suddenly and gestures for the others to wait. "That's odd," he whispers. "I think I recognise that voice ..." Ottoline listens too. "Never!" booms a second speaker. "How dare you threaten me?" "Zeph's father," murmurs Ottoline "but who's he talking to?" Rupert creeps forward and peers round the bottom of the stairs. "Billy Blizzard!" he gasps. "I thought it was him I could hear. Whatever is he doing here? And why has he made Zeph's father so cross?"

Rupert has met Billy Blizzard before, and wonders what Jack Frost's mischievous cousin can be up to ... inching forward, he is astonished to see the four winds, captured in fine gauze sacks. "He's holding them prisoner!" gasps Rupert and then listens carefully as Billy repeats his demands. "From now on, you'll obey my orders!" he cries. "I'll send blizzards wherever I like, all year round, not only in the winter ... King Frost and the Weather Clerk thought they could banish me to the South Pole, but this time I'll show them."

Rupert hurries to tell the news,
They must stop Billy, no time to lose.

North Wind booms at the odd little man,
Thinking hard Rupert finds a plan.

To beat Billy will not be hard,
Baby wind can catch him off guard.

Upstairs Zeph flies, waits for a sign;
Hard he'll blow to ring the chime.

Rupert hurries back to warn Zeph and Ottoline. "Billy Blizzard's caught Zeph's parents," he whispers. "He plans to upset the whole World's weather!" "I'll never obey you!" booms the North Wind. "Then you'll stay where you are forever," jeers Billy in reply. "We've got to stop him!" gasps Ottoline. "Yes," says Rupert. "But how? If he knows we're here, he'll try and catch us too ..." Thinking hard for a moment, Rupert suddenly has an idea. "Zeph!" he cries. "The one wind Billy's forgotten ..."

Rupert tells Ottoline the only way they can beat Billy Blizzard is to catch him off guard. "He's so sure he's caught all the winds that he won't be expecting another one to arrive ..." As Rupert explains his plan, Zeph listens carefully, then flies up towards a huge set of wind chimes that hang by the stairs. "Wait for my sign," says Rupert. "We're about to give Billy a big surprise ..." As the baby wind hovers above, the two chums scramble for cover. "Good!" Says Rupert. "He'll never spot us here."

RUPERT

causes a distraction

*With the chums hidden, off Zeph goes
And all around the noise echoes.*

*Surprised, Billy comes rushing out.
"I'll catch you, too!" they hear him shout.*

*From their hiding place come the pair,
To free the winds from their despair.*

*The Clerk thought there was something wrong;
Thank goodness that Rupert came along.*

As soon as the chums are ready, Rupert waves to Zeph then ducks down under the stairs. The baby wind smiles, then starts ringing the chimes as loudly as he can. A noisy jangling shatters the quiet of the tower, which echoes all around. Almost at once, an astonished Billy Blizzard comes running out to see what is happening. "Who's there?" he demands. "I've caught all the winds." Zeph rings the chimes again, then flits away. "I'll catch you too," cries Billy and hurries upstairs after him ...

Rupert and Ottoline stay hidden under the staircase until Billy has gone. "Now!" calls Rupert. "Follow me." Hurrying across the hall, he runs to where the winds are still tied up in sacks. "Wh ... who are you?" blinks Zeph's mother. "How did you ring the chimes?" "We've come from the Weather Clerk," says Rupert. "He thought there must be something wrong and sent us along to see ..." "Thanks goodness," sighs the South Wind. "Billy Blizzard tricked us all and now won't let us go." "Villain!" scowls her husband.

RUPERT
unties all the winds

Each wind in sacks, tied so tightly!
"We'll get you free," says Rupert brightly.

But Billy's back and his device
Will turn the two pals into ice.

Evil Billy prepares to throw
The powder, but Zeph starts to blow.

The dust makes Billy start to sneeze,
They must hurry so he can't freeze.

Each of the winds is caught in a sack that is tightly tied with a drawstring. "Don't worry," says Rupert. "We'll soon set you free ..." "I wouldn't be too sure of that," snaps an angry voice. "Billy Blizzard!" gasps Rupert. "I might have know it was you," cries Billy. "You're always interfering with my plans. This time I'll turn you into a block of ice." Opening the pouch on his belt, he takes a handful of powder and laughs. "Your friend can join you," he cackles. "I've nothing to fear from a pair of statues."

Billy Blizzard is just about to throw the freezing powder at Rupert when Zeph swoops into the room. With a cry of alarm, he darts to Rupert's side and blows a mighty puff of wind, which covers Billy in a cloud of dust. Sneezing and gasping with surprise, he turns away, just long enough for Rupert and Ottoline to act. "See if you can untie Zeph's parents," calls Rupert. "I'll release the others ..." "Hurry!" calls the West Wind. "As soon as that rascal recovers, he'll try to freeze you again."

33

RUPERT

saves the day

"I'll teach you," Billy says at last,
But what he sees then makes him gasp.

The winds are free, he must escape
And get out of this nasty scrape.

As Billy shouts out, "Let me go ..."
Around him a whirlwind they all blow.

The wind swirls, his balance is lost,
Off to the dungeon of King Frost.

Billy Blizzard stops sneezing and turns to face Rupert and Ottoline. "I'll teach you to meddle with my plans!" he cries, then stops with a sudden gasp. "You've freed the winds!" "Exactly," says Zeph's uncle. "Thanks to Rupert, your plot's been thwarted." "You're the one who needs a lesson," cries his brother. "Stop!" wails Billy. "I didn't mean it really. I only wanted to make a point. I would have let you go ..." "Liar!" scowls the wind. Billy dashes to the door and escapes outside.

Zeph's uncles race out after Billy, then fly round and round him, faster and faster. "They're making a whirlwind," gasps Rupert. "Let me go!" yells Billy but the winds only laugh. "You're our prisoner now," calls the West Wind. "We'll blow you wherever we like." The pair fly higher and higher, until Billy is swept out to sea. "Where are they taking him?" asks Ottoline. "To King Frost's dungeons," says Zeph's mother. "And that's where he can stay."

When Zeph was lost nobody knew
Where to look or what they should do.

South Wind was caught in his captor's net,
But about Zeph, Billy Blizzard did forget.

"Zeph heard my chimes," says Ottoline,
"He came to Nutwood just in time."

At the tower Billy lurked and waited,
The winds were all fooled they stated.

"Thanks goodness you found little Zeph," says the South Wind. "I was so worried when we got separated and nobody knew where he was ..." "What happened?" asks Rupert. "How did Billy Blizzard catch you?" "In a net," says the wind. "Zeph and I were flying along together when we suddenly came to a patch of cloud. Billy was hidden from sight and trapped me before I knew he was there." "What about Zeph?" asks Ottoline. "He flew on alone," explains the wind. "Billy Blizzard forgot all about him."

"So that's how Zeph got lost," says Ottoline. "Nutwood must have been the first village he came to. I expect my wind chimes reminded him of home ..." "Just as well he didn't fly back to the tower," nods the North Wind. "That rascal Blizzard was waiting to trap us all, one by one. As soon as I flew in through my porthole he caught me in his net and tied it with a string ..." Zeph's father scowls at the thought of Billy's plan. "Blizzards all year round!" he scoffs. "The very idea."

There's lots of work to catch up on
Agree the winds, so let's be gone.

The chums are ready to return,
Fair winds will help them home they learn.

The Weather Clerk hurries to greet,
"Well done," he cries as they all meet.

Billy's plan was against all reason;
Snow should only fall in the correct season.

Now that Zeph is safely home, Rupert and Ottoline can fly back and tell the Weather Clerk what has been happening ... "We'll come with you," says the North Wind. "There'll be lots of work to catch up on: rain clouds to deliver and washing to be dried; ships to sail and cool breezes needed ..." The chums climb into the cloud hopper and are soon on their way. "A fair wind to fly by," calls Zeph's mother and blows them on their way. "Hurrah!" laughs Ottoline. "We'll be there in no time at all ..."

The moment the cloud-hopper touches down, a door opens and the Weather Clerk comes hurrying out. "Well done!" he cries. "You've found Zeph's parents I see." "More than that," calls the North Wind. "They've rescued us as well!" "Rescued?" blinks the Clerk. He frowns as he hears how Billy planned to send blizzards all year round. "Don't worry," says Zeph's father, "There is plenty of snow for Billy to play with in the North Pole in King Frost's dungeon!"

Now it's time to say their goodbyes,
Down to the chums little Zeph flies.

"Come back to Nutwood soon," they say,
"We'll fly our kite again and play."

The lever is pulled, a gentle glide,
Suddenly there is a rainbow slide.

The chums climb on with cries of glee,
"It's home we go," they both shout "Wheee!"

Before the winds leave, Zeph flutters down to say goodbye to Rupert and Ottoline. "Do come back to Nutwood soon," smiles Ottoline. "We can all fly kites together." The winds head off together flying up high into the sky. "Well," says the Weather Clerk, "It is time you were heading back to Nutwood now," declares the Clerk. He leads the chums to a platform at the side of the Weather Station and then tells them to wait.

"A rainbow!" gasps Ottoline as the Clerk pulls a lever. "Yes," smiles the Clerk. "A rainbow slide. I can make it end wherever I want to from here." Thanking the pair for all their help, he tells them to climb on to the rainbow and slide down. "Wheee!" cries Rupert, "What fun." " Like a huge helter-skelter," laughs Ottoline. They both happily slide down the rainbow, which ends in the middle of Nutwood common, where the whole adventure started.

THE END

Spot the Difference

Here are two pictures which at first glance look identical. However, there are actually 10 differences between the two. Can you find them all? *Answers can be found on page 109.*

RUPERT
and the
Sum Bean

John Harrold.

RUPERT
wonders what is wrong

Mr Bear is shaking his head,
"Something's wrong with spring," he said.

Plants that should be in full bloom
Are still locked deep in winter's gloom.

Going to school Rupert sees
Some confusion among the trees.

In a leafless branch a cuckoo
Who says the birds don't know what to do!

Mr Bear is already out in the garden as Rupert sets off for school one morning. He is looking around and shaking his head. "What has gone wrong with spring?" he sighs. "Everything is happening in the wrong order. Look at this, Rupert. The grass is growing strongly again, yet by the look of those bare shrubs over there you'd think it's still winter. This little plant here should be in bloom – but no sign of anything on it. Yet those roses which should not bloom for several weeks are almost ready."

On his way to school Rupert can see all around him signs that everything does seem to be happening in the wrong order this spring. The trees where the crows nest look almost summery. Yet the ones he is just passing are winter-bare. The same goes for hedges, flowers and plants. On the leafless branch of one tree two puzzled cuckoos are perched. Rupert hears one of them complaining. "I simply don't know whether we should be cuckooing or not." "What can have gone wrong?" Rupert wonders.

RUPERT
finds a bead

Spring can be early, it can be late,
But he's not known one with this fate.

Just then on the path Rupert sees
A strangely odd but little bead.

To use the bead he has a ploy,
With it he can repair a toy.

A counting frame Rupert will mend
And to Bill Badger he will send

Rupert is still wondering about this odd spring as he goes on his way to school. "I've known spring early and I've known it late," he muses. "But never all mixed up and out of order!" Just then he sees something on the path. It looks like a bead, and when he picks it up he finds it does have a hole pierced through it. Yet, though it's hard, it doesn't feel like an ordinary bead somehow. Then as he studies it he sees how he might use it and pockets it. On a nearby branch a squirrel watches all this.

That evening Rupert shows his find to Mrs Bear and tells her how he plans to use it. From the back of his toy cupboard he has dug out what's left of a small counting frame he had when he was very small. "When it got broken one of the beads was lost," he says. "If this one I've found fits the counting frame I'll mend it and give it to Bill Badger for his little brother." Mrs Bear thinks that is a splendid idea, so Rupert tries out his new bead, finds that it fits and starts to rebuild the counting frame.

He works so hard to mend the frame,
Though not as strong, it is the same.

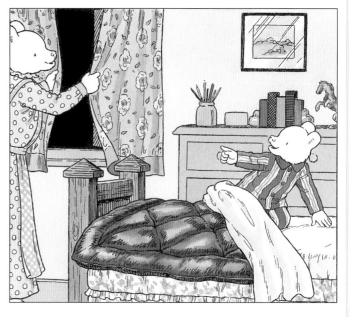

Open the window he suggests,
Mrs Bear agrees to this request.

As Rupert a deep sleep enjoys
Wakes with a start at a sudden noise.

Rupert shouts, raises the alarm.
It was a dream, there is no harm.

Right up to supper-time Rupert works at repairing his old counting frame. "It looks really fine," Mr Bear says when the job is done. "But you'd better tell Bill to make sure his little brother doesn't treat it roughly. It isn't likely to be as strong as it was." Mrs Bear fetches wrapping paper and string, saying that she will wrap the frame when Rupert has gone to bed. Later as Rupert climbs into bed he asks if his window can be left a little open since it is so mild. "Of course, dear," Mrs Bear smiles.

Rupert has not long been asleep when he is awakened by a noise like something being dropped near him. "Mummy!" he cries. In the seconds it takes Mr and Mrs Bear to reach him there is a flurry of his curtains as if something has gone through the open window. Mr Bear looks out but can see nothing. "You must have dreamt it," says Mrs Bear. "Then how did my box that had the counting beads in it get on the floor?" Rupert asks. "Likely because you didn't put it away properly, silly," smiles Mrs Bear. "Now, back to sleep."

RUPERT

is captured

Next day Rupert sets off and blinks,
Maybe it was a dream, he thinks.

In the trees where the bead he found,
Sudden darkness, a rustling sound.

Rupert struggles but small hands grip.
Just who would play this kind of trick?

He's pushed along, and hears a hiss
The blanket falls, who is behind this?

By next morning Rupert is beginning to feel that maybe he did dream someone got into his bedroom and disturbed his toy cupboard. So he's not his usual cheerful self when he sets off for school with the mended counting frame in a parcel. As he goes he thinks, "Bill's little brother will be glad to have it. But Bill must warn him that it isn't as strong as it was." He is near where he found the bead when there is a rustle in the branches overhead and suddenly he is wrapped in darkness.

Rupert struggles to throw off the sheet or blanket that has been dropped on him. But small strong hands grip him and he has to give up. His mind is in a whirl. What? Who? Why? No-one he knows would play this sort of trick. Not even the Fox brothers. The small hands urge him along – quite gently as if they didn't want to hurt him, but very firmly. A halt. Rustling. Creaking. Then Rupert feels himself being led down steps. Another halt. The blanket is removed. Facing him is someone he recognises.

He is before the Imps' King
It is their job to awaken spring.

"Where is our Bean?" he says with gloom,
"We did not find it in your room."

Now Rupert knows what it's about,
"I found your Sum Bean," he shouts.

"I put it on my counting frame,"
"It fell down when your Imps came."

"The Imps' King!" breathes Rupert. More than once on his adventures Rupert has met the ruler of the Imps of Spring, the tiny creatures whose job is to waken the countryside after its winter sleep. But he has never seen him look so stern. "Where is our Sum Bean?" the King demands. "Sunbeam?" Rupert asks. "No, Sum Bean," the King repeats. "I don't know what you mean!" Rupert protests. "A squirrel saw you find it," the King retorts. "But my Imps could not find it when they searched your room last night."

Now Rupert sees! There was someone in his room last night. And he knows what the King is talking about. "Your Sum Bean must be the bead I found!" He cries. "It didn't feel like an ordinary one." "Well, what did you think I was talking about?" snaps the King. "Where is it?" "On my counting frame," Rupert begins. Then he pauses. "Oh dear," he says, "I dropped it when your Imps grabbed me." "What?" the King yells. "Everyone, outside at once and find that counting frame!" There is a rush to obey.

RUPERT
learns of the Sum Bean

Rupert is caught up in the rush,
The frame has gone, there's a sudden hush.

"It's so important, tell me why?"
"I need your help," the King does sigh.

The King explains about the Bean,
A vital part of their machine.

It's old and worn and spring's gone wrong.
A new one's ordered and now it's gone.

Rupert is caught in the rush of Imps to search for his counting frame and the Sum Bean. Even the King joins in the dash up to the outside world. The Imps who trapped Rupert lead the way to the spot. But the parcel containing the counting frame is not to be seen. Every place it might have been knocked or kicked to is searched. But no. Not a sign of it. "Why is the Sum Bean so important?" Rupert asks. The King thinks then speaks: "I want your help to find it so I shall tell you."

The King posts an Imp lookout on a branch before explaining to Rupert: "Getting spring started means getting so many things going in the right order. To work out that order we use a machine, and its most important part is the Sum Bean. This year everything began to happen in the wrong order. Our Sum Bean had worn out! We ordered another from the Sum Bean grower. Alas, the messenger bringing it lost it through a hole in his pouch. It was the grower's last one! It must be found and you must help us to find it."

RUPERT
offers to help the Imps

Rupert goes, his parents to tell.
To call the Imps, his name he'll yell.

"So that's what's wrong!" says Mr Bear,
"We all must look, we'll do our share."

As he walks he looks around
But not a sparkler anywhere is found.

The postman sees that Rupert's late,
"Hurry now, to the school gate!"

Before leaving, Rupert promises the King he will do all he can to find the Sum Bean and will tell only his parents about it. He is also told how to contact the Imps if he must. He is to come to where they trapped him and call "Rupert" twice. That evening Rupert tells his parents about the lost Sum Bean. When they have both said "So, that's what's wrong!" Mr Bear suggests that Rupert ask his pals if they have come across the counting frame. "Mummy and I will keep our eyes and ears open too," he says.

Rupert decides to keep his eyes open for the counting frame on his way to school next day. After all, it could have ended up anywhere ... So when he sees anything that might be a parcel he investigates, peering into ditches and under hedges. He even asks the postman if he has seen anything like it. The postman is surprised to see Rupert. He looks at his watch and asks: "Are you going to school?" When Rupert says he is, the postman tells him, "Well, you had better get a move on. You're terribly late already."

Rupert runs with all his might,
At the school there's no one in sight.

"Oh, please sir," he begins to say.
The Fox brothers are in his way.

They are praised; it's a rare sight,
The only ones to get all the sums right.

"Do you have a counting machine?"
Asks Dr Chimp, with a beam.

Rupert runs as fast as he can the rest of the way to school. But when he gets there the playground is empty. School has begun. Rupert has never been so late. He makes his way to the classroom and edges through the doorway. Everyone turns to look. "Oh, please Sir," he begins. But Dr Chimp the teacher halts him. "I'll hear what you have to say when I am finished with these two." In front of him stand the Fox brothers, Ferdy and Freddy. "What have they been up to?" Rupert wonders.

Rupert is astonished to learn that the Fox brothers are not in trouble – just for once! He hears Dr Chimp say "I know the homework sums were hard, but only Ferdy and Freddy got them right." No wonder Rupert is surprised. The Foxes are the stupidest pair in the class. "Plainly they have been working very hard" Dr Chimp goes on. "Or ..." and he gives a small smile which means he is making a joke "... they have some sort of counting machine". With a start Rupert sees the Fox brothers exchange a glance.

RUPERT
follows the Fox brothers

"The Foxes have the counting frame!"
Thinks Rupert as he plans his game.

He follows them back to their house,
Watches them, quiet as a mouse.

In the summerhouse Rupert sees,
The Foxes and their little wheeze.

A finger on the magic bean,
The answer to a sum they glean.

"The Foxes have the counting frame! For a moment they thought teacher had found them out when he joked about them having a counting machine!" The thoughts race through Rupert's mind. He feels so sure that he decides to follow the brothers home. So after school he lets them get a little ahead then follows. When they reach their house they go indoors. "Now what?" Rupert wonders. But in a few minutes they re-appear and make for a sort of summerhouse. They have their homework books with them.

Rupert steals into the garden and up to the summerhouse. He peeps through the window. Ferdy and Freddy, their backs to him, are sitting in front of his counting frame. He can hear them. "See if it's still working" Ferdy says. "Remember, we found you have to touch the odd-looking bead." Freddy puts a finger on the Sum Bean and recites a very hard sum from last night's homework. The beads flash back and forwards in a blur of speed. "Still working!" grins Ferdy. "We'll do our homework later."

Satisfied, Rupert slips away,
Knowing what the Foxes will say.

Hurries to the Imps of Spring.
"Please take me to see your King."

The King listens to Rupert's tale,
He has an idea on a clever scale.

He whispers what must happen now,
To return the bean is Rupert's vow.

Rupert slips away from the summerhouse before the Foxes emerge. Knowing the pair, he's quite sure they won't hand over the counting frame if he just asks - not now they know what it can do. So he decides to let the King of the Imps of Spring know he has traced the Sum Bean. He hurries to the place where the Imps trapped him and calls "Rupert" twice as he was told. In a twinkling the call is answered by Imps. "Take me to the King" Rupert demands. "I have very important news for him."

The King has ordered that Rupert be brought to him at once if he brings news of the Sum Bean. So in no time at all Rupert is reporting to the King. While he listens the King is thinking hard and when Rupert finishes he asks a strange question: "How strong is your counting frame?" When Rupert admits, "Not very," the King whispers an order to an Imp who hurries away to fetch something. Then he says to Rupert, "Here's what I want you to do ..." A little later Rupert leaves with a tiny packet.

RUPERT
surprises the Fox brothers

Back at the summerhouse he hides.
Empty the packet, he decides.

When their work the Foxes begin...
"That's mine," cries Rupert as he bursts in.

He makes a grab, the brothers fight,
Pull the frame with all their might.

The frame breaks, beads all scattered,
Rupert gets the one that mattered!

Rupert hurries to the Foxes garden, steals up to the summerhouse and peeps in. Good, it's empty! The brothers have not yet returned to do their homework. But he doesn't have to wait in hiding for long before they do appear. Now Rupert empties into his hand the little packet the King gave him. Then, as soon as the Foxes are in the summerhouse and before they can begin work, Rupert bursts in after them. "That's mine!" he cries, pointing at the counting frame. "And I'm taking it back!"

The Fox brothers are so startled that Rupert is able to make a grab for the counting frame before they act. Then they grab the counting frame too. "It's not yours!" yells Ferdy. "It is!" Rupert cries. They tug. He tugs – but with one hand only for the other is clenched. Tug! Tug! Crack! The frame breaks and beads scatter onto the floor. Rupert makes a dive for the Sum Bean. "He's got the special bead!" Freddy cries. "Get it!" Rupert on hands and knees, tucks his clenched hands under him.

50

RUPERT
gets the Sum Bean

Rupert puts out his fist clenched tight
Rupert thinks they may put up a fight!

Shoulders slumped, Rupert leaves.
His smiling face, no one sees.

Out of sight he starts to run.
Returns the Sum Bean, it's such fun.

"The Foxes now have the old one."
"I swapped them over, now it's done."

Rupert crouches with his clenched hands under him while the Fox brothers try to pull him to his feet. When they succeed, only one of Rupert's hands is clenched. "Hand it over – the special bead!" Ferdy demands. Rupert seems to hesitate for a moment then slowly opens his hand. Ferdy snatches the Sum Bean. "Now go away!" he orders Rupert. "It's our counting frame. We found it. And we'll soon mend it again." Shoulders slumped, the picture of defeat, Rupert leaves. The Foxes don't see the little smile on his face.

As soon as he is out of sight of the Fox brothers, Rupert breaks into a run. Not many minutes later he is summoning an Imp of Spring with his "Rupert" password and in no time handing the lost Sum Bean to the King. "The Foxes now have the old one you gave me – the one that makes awful mistakes," he says. "I switched them when the frame broke as you planned. I slipped the good new one in my pocket." "I feel almost sorry for those Foxes," the King says. But he is grinning as he speaks.

RUPERT
gets the counting frame back

Next day the Foxes are so glum,
Nothing right, not a single sum.

"Not one right sum will you two name,"
"If you use that counting frame!"

Within days spring behaves, as it should.
The Foxes return the frame for good.

"It's nothing but trouble," the Foxes say,
Rupert smiles as they walk away.

In school the next day the Foxes are again called to the front. "Only the Foxes ..." Dr Chimp begins and the pair smirk, "... got every homework sum hopelessly WRONG!" The Foxes cannot believe it. "You will do them again tonight," Dr Chimp snaps. As they return to their seats Rupert whispers, "You'll get them wrong again if you use that counting frame." "How do you know?" Ferdy hisses. "I can't say, but I do," Rupert replies. The Foxes look glummer than ever, for they know Rupert never tells fibs.

In a few days spring is here properly. Everything in the garden is as it should be. "The Imps wasted no time putting the new Sum Bean to work," Rupert is thinking when through the gate sidle the Foxes – with the counting frame. Ferdy thrusts it at Rupert. "Here!" he mutters. "It's done nothing but get us into trouble." As the pair turn away Rupert smiles and thinks "I'll have to get a bead to replace this dud Sum Bean!"

THE END

RUPERT
and the
Secret

John Harrold

RUPERT
has a visitor

One day a knock at Rupert's door comes
It's Billy Goat, one of the bear's chums.

The pals set off to make a visit
To Old Goat's castle, how far is it?

As the castle appears in sight
The pair rest up in warm sunlight.

Rupert delays to tie his lace
Billy goes on, his uncle to face.

One day, when Rupert is thinking that it is some time since he saw the Wise Old Goat, there comes a knock at the door and who should be on the step but Billy Goat, one of Rupert's chums, and a relative of the Wise Old Goat. "I'm off to stay with the Wise Old Goat for a couple of days," says Billy. "Would you like to come?" It's not long afterwards that Rupert and Billy, knapsacks on their backs are striding out towards the hills where the Wise Old Goat's castle lies. Ahead lies a hard slog but that doesn't worry them.

The sun is high by the time the Wise Old Goat's castle comes in sight and both Rupert and Billy are beginning to feel the effect of the long upward slog. When a convenient boulder turns up at the side of the track the pair perch themselves on it for a breather. As they rise to move off again Rupert notices that one of his laces is loose. "You go on," he tells Billy. "I'll tie this and catch you up." But he doesn't and Billy is some way ahead when they reach their destination.

RUPERT
hears Billy's cries

"I'll tell him that you're just behind!"
Shouts Billy hoping he won't mind.

On the step what does Rupert hear?
A cry of surprise, it sounds like fear.

From behind a bush Rupert peers,
He takes a breath to check his fears.

The urge to run is very strong
But he knows that would be so wrong.

"I'll tell him you're just behind me!" Billy turns in the doorway of the Wise Old Goat's castle and calls back to Rupert. Then he disappears inside. Rupert has reached the steps leading to the door when he stops in his tracks. From inside the castle comes a cry. It is a cry of surprise and fear: "Who are you? No, please ..." It is Billy. Rupert dashes after his chum. Then he checks himself. Whatever was waiting for Billy will be waiting for him!

Rupert ducks behind a nearby bush and peers fearfully at the doorway through which Billy disappeared. But there is no further sound from him and no-one appears. Rupert badly wants to make a run for it and even tells himself he ought to in order to get help. Then he takes a deep breath and decides, no, he must at least find out what's happened to his chum. Quite a time passes before he works up the courage to steal out and tiptoe into the Wise Old Goat's home.

RUPERT
tries to help his friends

Through the doorway Rupert tears,
He pauses and listens at the stairs.

Then a shock as he sees the pair
Billy and Goat tied to a chair.

A heavy hand his shoulder grips,
Pulls him so hard he nearly slips.

The captor smiles, he can't break free
A strange, black-bearded man is he.

Rupert pauses inside the doorway and holds his breath. Not a sign of anyone and he can almost feel the silence. "I must do something," he tells himself after standing motionless for what seems a long time. Then he sees that the door to the Wise Old Goat's workroom is open. He steals towards it, peeks in ... gasps. Billy and the Wise Old Goat are there, trussed to chairs and gagged. Without thinking he dashes towards them. Eyes rolling they shake their heads desperately.

Too late Rupert realises that Billy and the Wise Old Goat are trying to warn him of something. As he passes through the open door of the Goat's workshop a heavy hand falls on his shoulder and almost jerks him off his feet. He struggles and squirms but he cannot break free. Then he finds himself picked up and plonked down on a workbench. Now he sees his captor, a strangely garbed man with a black beard and an unpleasant smile. "Yes, you'll do," he sneers.

RUPERT
hears of the 'Nutwood Secret'

Scared of his captor, Rupert quavers,
The man's demand never wavers.

The Nutwood Secret is his aim
Among Wizards it has much fame.

"Down the well is a secret chest,"
Rupert, he says must do his best.

A fearsome sword is at his waist;
Rupert is scared and acts with haste.

"You are going to fetch the Nutwood Secret for me," the man tells Rupert. "I've never heard of any Nutwood Secret," Rupert quavers. "I have!" the man snaps. "I am Warlock. I mix with wizards and sorcerers and for years I have heard them mention this Nutwood Secret. No one knows what it is. But plainly it must be valuable, for over the years, I have learned that it lies in a chest at the bottom of a dry well in this very house and that the Wise Old Goat is its guardian."

"What do you want me to do?" Rupert asks. "Go down the well for the chest which contains the secret ... just in case there's some sort of trap," says the man. Rupert looks at the Old Wise Goat who shakes his head. "No, no!" Rupert stammers. The man's response is to pull aside his tunic to reveal a ferocious sword at his waist. "You shall," he says coldly. "Or it will be the worse for your friends." Seconds later Rupert is being marched into a little courtyard containing a well.

RUPERT
is ordered down the well

Warlock's had time to make ready,
Rupert must keep his nerve steady.

A rope around his waist is tied
Give three tugs once the chest is spied.

As he's lowered into the well
On dark thoughts he starts to dwell.

"When I've found and tied on the chest,"
"To go back with it will be best."

Plainly Warlock has been in the Wise Old Goat's home long enough to have found the well and made his arrangements. For beside the well are a lantern and a crowbar which he uses to prise off a metal grille sealing off the well. Then he lifts Rupert on to the low wall of the well, ties the bucket rope around his waist and hands him the lighted lantern. "When you find the chest send it up on the rope." Says Warlock. "Then I'll send the rope down again for you."

Rupert is ready to be lowered into the well. He has been told to tug twice on the rope when he reaches the bottom then three times when he has tied the chest to it. It will be pulled up then the rope returned for him. He says nothing as Warlock starts to lower him but thinks, "If I do find the chest down here I'm coming up with it. I just know he means to leave me in the well." The light from the well-head dwindles and only the lantern's glow pierces the deep gloom.

RUPERT
finds a treasure chest

Rupert stumbles and goes sprawling
But sees something just as he's falling.

Without light he can't see at all
But the lantern shows the chest is small.

"What on earth can the secret be?"
"Can that small chest be the key?"

For treasure it just looks too small,
Rupert glances around at the wall.

Just when Rupert's beginning to think there's no bottom to this well, his feet touch something solid. He tugs the rope as he's been told. Very carefully he settles on to the solid surface, takes a cautious step ahead ... and goes sprawling. Whatever it was he came down on it was higher than the bottom of the well. Rupert picks himself up and turns the lantern on the thing. "The chest!" he gasps. "Why it's much smaller than I though it was going to be."

Rupert stands looking at the chest in the light of his lantern and he thinks, "does that little chest really contain the Nutwood Secret? What on earth can it be? If it's a treasure hoard then it's a pretty small one as treasure hoards go". Remember, more than once in his adventures Rupert has come across treasure hoards, usually pirates', and they've always been in much bigger chests. Before lifting it he sweeps the beam from his lantern around the well shaft, and sees something strange.

He sees a door, it has no latch
And wonders if there is a catch.

It will not budge, there is no hope
Rupert steps back and tugs the rope.

Warlock starts to wind him higher
And is exposed as one big liar!

He would have left poor Rupert there
Now he is shocked to see the bear.

What Rupert has seen is a low doorway set into an arch. Cautiously, he goes towards it. It has no latch or handle, and has the look of a door that hasn't been open for ages and ages. Rupert pushes it gently. Nothing. He pushes as hard as he can. Nothing. Somehow he is relieved that it hasn't opened. He backs away from it and picks up the chest. It is much lighter than he expected. He clasps it to his chest with one hand and the other tugs the rope three times.

The rope tightens as Warlock starts to wind it up. Rupert feels himself start to rise. "Thank you, little bear!" Warlock's voice rings mockingly down the well shaft. "Perhaps one day we shall meet again ..." "A lot sooner than you think," Rupert mutters angrily. Gradually the well shaft gets lighter. Is Warlock going to look down and see Rupert? No, he's too busy winding up what he thinks is the chest containing the Nutwood Secret. Now Rupert's head appears above the top of the well.

Warlock shouts an angry bellow
When he sees the little fellow.

"I'll drop the chest," does Rupert yell
So Warlock backs off from the well.

He sways the rope and grabs the wall;
Not Rupert or the chest will fall.

Warlock leaps back in one bound,
He thinks the Secret now is found.

"You!" Warlock lets out an outraged bellow as he straightens and sees Rupert, "Y-you've cheated. You said you'd wait down there ..." Rupert retorts. "I just knew you meant to leave me there." "Well, back down the well's where you're going!" snarls Warlock. "Stand back!" cries Rupert. "Touch me and I'll drop this chest down the well!" For a moment Warlock looks as if he is about to lunge. Then he backs away from the well-head.

When he feels Warlock is far enough away Rupert sways the rope over to the well-head wall and pulls himself to safety. While he loosens the rope from around himself Rupert puts the chest on the wall. It is then Warlock bounds forward and snatches up the chest with a cry of triumph. The tool he used to remove the well-head grille is lying nearby. He grabs it and sets about prising open the chest. The ancient lock snaps. The lid is raised. Warlock peers in – and gives a great cry.

RUPERT
has a plan!

Grabbing Rupert's right hand tightly
Warlock drags him, none too lightly!

"There's no treasure," he exclaims
"Just a key in the chest," he explains.

Warlock rants and threatens them all.
Rupert sees something by the wall.

It's Wise Old Goat's clock time machine
Now, to trick Warlock who is so mean.

Warlock bangs shut the chest, and grabbing Rupert by the hand drags him indoors and into the room where Billy and the Wise Old Goat sit trussed and gagged. Roughly he ungags the Wise Old Goat. "There is no treasure in the chest at the bottom of your well," he snarls. "Is this, then, your Nutwood Secret?" And from the chest he takes ... a key. The Goat is silent. "Or is it ..." he pauses. "... The key to the Secret, the treasure?" The Goat says nothing. But Rupert starts to have an idea.

Warlock is sure he has the key to the Nutwood Secret – a treasure of some sort, he's convinced. But what does the key open? He has no idea and the Wise Old Goat is not telling. While Warlock rants and threatens, Rupert is thinking hard. He eyes what looks like a grandfather clock inside a glass case. It is the Goat's History Clock, a machine that more than once has carried Rupert back and forward in time. "Oh sir," he cries, "That clock isn't what it seems."

RUPERT
tricks Warlock

The clock is not the Secret, true,
But for this purpose it will do.

Set the numbers one-nought-six-six
And we'll soon have him in a fix.

Rupert slams shut the clock's glass case
A confused look passes Warlock's face.

Rupert turns the time machine on;
Warlock fades and then he is gone.

"That clock does not contain the Nutwood Secret!" cries the Wise Old Goat. That's true, but Warlock only sneers and advances on the History Clock. "It won't work unless you set the hands to the right number," Rupert says. And that's true, too. For that way you set the year you want to travel to. "It's one-nought-six-six," Rupert says, picking the first number he thinks of. Warlock steps into the case surrounding the clock. He sets the hands. Rupert slams the case door.

The glass case around the History Clock is there to ensure that no one gets carried off in time by accident, as happened once to Rupert. Warlock turns at the sound of the door being shut. But the moment he needs to take in what's happening is enough for Rupert to leap to the wall-switch that operates the Clock and turn it on. Warlock wrestles with the unfamiliar glass door, but even as he does his image fades and dwindles and he is on his way back through the centuries.

A sharp knife cuts the ropes that tie,
The trick has worked, he did not lie.

Threats Warlock would have carried out
Of that Wise Old Goat has no doubt.

Rupert spots the key on the floor
He's anxious to know what it's for.

"Is it for the door in the well?"
Wise Old Goat knows, but he won't tell.

As soon as he has ungagged Billy Goat, Rupert hurries to the kitchen to fetch a sharp knife and cut his friend free. "That was a very quick bit of thinking on your part, Rupert," says the Wise Old Goat. "I don't doubt that awful Warlock was quite ready to carry out his awful threats. Being dumped back in history is no more than he deserved." "Well, we did tell him the truth." Rupert says. "I said the Clock wasn't what it seemed and you told him it didn't contain the Nutwood Secret."

"The key!" Rupert and the others are enjoying tea when Rupert remembers Warlock was holding the key when he vanished. "I'm sure I saw him drop it when he tried to get out." And yes, sure enough, there on the floor of the case around the History Clock lies the little old key. "I'll find a safe place for it," says the Wise Old Goat. "Does it open that little door at the bottom of the well?" Rupert dares to ask. The Wise Old Goat smiles and says nothing.

Next day the pals prepare to go
What the Secret is, they still don't know.

Wise Old Goat says that is the way,
To keep it a secret it must stay.

The Secret that's not safe to tell
Remains in hiding down the well.

But you, dear reader, can be told
The Great Goats turned nuts into gold!

Next morning and time for Billy and Rupert to leave for home. "You've been very good about not asking what the Nutwood Secret is," says the Wise Old Goat. "If I told you, it would no longer be a secret. But this much I will tell you, it's nothing dreadful. But it is a secret best kept that way." As the pals tramp homeward Rupert chuckles. "Well at least we can have fun inventing things the Secret might be!"

"I couldn't tell Rupert and Billy what the Secret is. They're Nutwooders. But I can tell you. My kind, the Great Goats, were Nutwood's first inhabitants – so wise they could make gold from nuts. But they knew such knowledge in the hands of others could cause awful harm. So they hid the secret formula ... behind that door at the bottom of the well – where the key is going again."

THE END

RUPERT

"Rupert's better," the doctor says,
A cough has kept him in for days.

"I think your Rupert is quite better now," Dr Lion tells Mrs Bear. "I certainly feel all right," says Rupert, who has been stuck indoors for days with a nasty cough. "It's only a pity you can't get away some place warm for a bit," says the doctor looking out at the still wintry scene. "Mr Jack!" Rupert gasps as Mrs Bear ushers a caller in. "Well, well!" says the newcomer. "I was sorry to learn from my brother the Professor that you haven't been well. You see, I hoped you might be able to join me on an expedition I'm just about to start on ..."

A knock at the door, someone's there,
"It's Mr Jack," says Mrs Bear.

The visitor explains his scheme,
An expedition is his theme.

"Is it to somewhere warm?" asks Dr Lion. "Oh yes," Mr Jack tells him. "It's to the Southern Sea." "Oh, then that's just what the doctor ordered – or suggested anyway!" Dr Lion laughs. "A break somewhere warm would do Rupert a power of good. I do recommend it, Mrs Bear." "Oh, dear, um, well, yes, if you say so?" Mrs Bear stammers. "May he fly doctor?" asks Mr Jack. "Certainly," the doctor says. "Ooh, great!" Rupert cries.

"Are you going to somewhere warm?"
"I think his health this may reform!"

RUPERT

The legend of Golden Apples Jack has found,
And to the Southern Sea he is bound.

In the harvicopter they will fly,
Sucking the apples right into the sky.

Rupert's waiting, clothes in a pack,
Waving he drives off with Mr Jack

The Professor at the tower is standing by,
Near the machine in which they'll fly.

"I have come into possession of an old map," says Mr Jack. "This shows golden apples growing on an island in the Southern Sea. I'm flying there in my brother's harvicopter and I could use a helper – like Rupert." "I've flown in the harvicopter!" cries Rupert. "Your brother invented it to gather fruit by air, but it made mush of the fruit." "My brother has fixed that," Mr Jack says. "It will safely suck up the few golden apples I want for seed to grow at home. Now, I will collect you first thing in the morning for our expedition."

Rupert is ready and waiting, his case packed, by the time Mr Jack arrives. "Now don't you worry," Mr Jack tells Rupert's parents. "He'll be perfectly all right and the trip will do him good." So the two set off by car to the tower home of the Professor, Mr Jack's brother and Rupert's clever old friend. The Professor is waiting by his flying harvester, the harvicopter. "All's set, chaps," he says. "Got the map Jack? Good. Then just point yourselves in the right direction."

All is ready, and goodbyes said,
The harvicopter flies off overhead.

Soon Nutwood is lost in a haze,
The pals fly on to warmer days.

On the map there is a feature,
A drawing of a strange, odd creature.

Above the island a griffin stands.
Rupert cries out as he spies land.

All is ready. Goodbyes are said. The harvicopter's engine is started. Snug in his warm coat in the rear cockpit, Rupert waves to the Professor, and then they're off. In no time Nutwood is lost in the wintry haze and the expedition to the island of the Golden Apples has begun. On and on our two fly over the mountains and oceans towards the warmth of the Southern Sea. Before he has finished the last of his sandwiches, Rupert has had to wriggle out of his warm coat.

"We should be seeing the island soon," says Mr Jack after a while. "If this chart is right," he adds. Rupert looks over Mr Jack's shoulder at the chart he has propped up before him. "What's that?" he asks pointing to a drawing of a strange creature above the island on the map. "That's a griffin," says Mr Jack. "The ancients believed in them, but of course, they didn't really exist any more than real gold apples did." Rupert peers ahead. "I say," he cries, "there is an island now!"

It is the isle they're looking for,
No sign of a soul on the shore.

But from the cockpit Rupert peeks,
Is that a vessel in the creek?

Now Mr Jack cries out with glee,
"I think we've found the golden tree."

To their surprise the tree stands tall
Surrounded by a garden wall.

"Yes, it's our island all right!" Mr Jack cries. "Just where the chart says and looking just as I've read about it in ancient books. And no sign of a soul on the place." "Probably because it's such a long way from anywhere," thinks Rupert. But wait! What's that? By now they are over the island and he is sure he caught a glimpse of some sort of vessel tucked away in a well-wooded creek. "Probably someone stopped off for fresh water," Mr Jack suggests when Rupert tells him.

Rupert is about to suggest they take a closer look at the vessel he glimpsed when Mr Jack cries, "I think we've found one – a golden apples tree! But, Rupert look!" The harvicopter is now hovering over the highest point on the island. Rupert looks down to where Mr Jack is pointing and gasps. There, sure enough, is a gnarled old tree with golden glintings amongst its dense foliage. But it is standing by itself in what looks like a walled garden! Whose garden? And whose is the tree?

Nothing about this in the book,
They'd better take a closer look.

The vehicle lands, the pals alight,
But no one seems to be in sight.

It's odd, the apples are up so high.
To climb up, Rupert's keen to try.

Just take a look, the pals agree,
So Rupert scampers up the tree.

"This is something the map and books didn't tell us," cries Mr Jack. "That tree must belong to whoever built the wall. So we can't simply suck up a few apples with the harvicopter. We shall have to find the owner and ask. Hang on, I'm going to land." Since the 'garden' is the only clear ground about, Mr Jack puts the harvicopter down inside the wall. Rupert and he climb out. No-one seems to be around. Curiously, there is no glinting gold in the tree to be seen from down here.

"Now that's odd," says Mr Jack. "There seem to be some apples high in the tree but none down here." "Shall I climb up and pick one?" asks Rupert. "Oh, no!" Mr Jack says. "We must find the owner and ask him – but you might climb up, have a look and tell me what they're like." So Rupert, who is a very good climber, starts up the tree. It is dim among the branches, with little light filtering through the dense canopy of leaves. But, look, there is something gleaming and gold just ahead.

71

He sees an apple, reaches out,
Touches it twice then gives a shout.

The apple's really made of gold,
A beak appears; he loses hold.

Rupert falls but to no harm,
Both fall down then look up in alarm!

A lion's body but wings of a bird,
It's the creature of which they heard ...

Rupert edges nearer to the gleaming apple. He stretches a hand for it. His fingers touch it – and he pulls them back with a startled cry. Then he puts out his hand and touches it again. "Mr Jack," he shouts, "Mr Jack, these apples really are gold. Real metal gold!" Then he breaks off with a cry of terror. For the canopy of leaves above him has parted and glaring at him is a fierce, beaked face. It screeches and as it does Rupert loses his grip and falls.

It's lucky for Rupert that Mr Jack is standing right under him and is quick-witted enough to catch him as he falls out of the tree. But they both end up sprawled flat. Before they can get up, something swoops out of the branches, lands beside them and looms over them with wings spread. The pair goggle at the creature. For, though it has the beak, talons and wings of a great bird, it has a lion's body! "It's the thing on the map!" breathes Rupert. "A griffin! The thing you say never existed!"

The griffin is guardian to the apples golden,
But half of them have now been stolen!

He lay in wait to catch the thieves,
The pals' story he just can't believe.

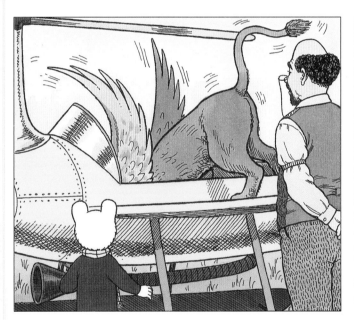

He starts to search inside the plane,
But his search for apples is in vain.

"If we'd flown in you would have heard,"
Says Mr Jack, "It is absurd."

"Are you really a g-griffin?" Rupert quavers. "You can see perfectly well I am!" fumes the creature. "And as the ancient guardian of the golden apples I have been waiting for you to return those you couldn't carry away with you. When I found half of them gone this morning I suspected you'd be back and so I lay in wait." "But we didn't take any golden apples!" chorus Rupert and Mr Jack. "You can search our aircraft," Mr Jack offers. "Oh, that I shall!" declares the griffin grimly.

The griffin ushers Mr Jack and Rupert over to their machine. "No tricks!" it warns and leaps into the cockpit where the others can hear it rummaging. It reappears and jumps down. "They're not there," it admits, "But that means nothing. You could have hidden them somewhere." "Look," reasons Mr Jack, "If we'd come and stolen the apples you'd have heard our flying machine. It's noisy enough." For a moment the griffin seems impressed. Then it shakes its head.

tells of the boat

"We didn't know they were real gold!"
But the griffin just won't be told.

The griffin has not seen the boat,
Although on the sea it was afloat.

Rupert says, "We could show it to you,"
"If over the island we all flew?"

To their plan, the griffin does agree,
"But," he says, "Rupert flies with me."

"Oh, please believe us!" begs Rupert. "Truly we did not steal the golden apples. We didn't even know they were real gold." Mr Jack nods vigorously. Rupert gets the idea that the griffin wants to believe them. But something's stopping it. It pauses. Then it says: "It must be you. There is no-one else on the island." The others exchange glances. "Do you have a boat?" Rupert asks. "A boat!" echoes the griffin. "No, I don't!" "Then there is someone else on the island!" Rupert cries. Rupert tells of the boat he glimpsed when he and Mr Jack arrived.

"I'm sure if we flew over the island I could show you where I saw it." The griffin nods. "Good," says Mr Jack. "Rupert and I will go in the harvicopter. Just follow ..." "Oh no!" the griffin grips Rupert's shoulder. "Your small friend will fly with me, just in case the two of you try to make a break for it!" So Mr Jack takes his place in the harvicopter and starts the engine. As the machine rises, so does the griffin. It hovers over Rupert then gently but firmly grasps him and lifts him clear of the ground. Its fierce-looking talons are surprisingly gentle.

RUPERT

"Stay well clear," orders Mr Jack.
"Don't you worry," griffin shouts back.

The path they came on they retrace.
Can Rupert find again that place?

Worriedly Rupert scans the coast,
It's proof the griffin needs the most.

At last he thinks he sees the creek.
Griffin swoops low to take a peek.

"Stay well back clear of the rotors!" Mr Jack calls to the griffin, pointing to the blades whirling above his head. "Do not worry about me or your small friend," the griffin calls back, and takes up a position behind and above the harvicopter well clear of the machine's slipstream. "Now, lead on!" it orders. The harvicopter moves off, retracing the path by which it first crossed the island, since it was then that Rupert glimpsed the mysterious vessel. Can he find it again?

Anxiously, Rupert scans the coast they are approaching. They must find that boat. It is the only proof that there has been someone else on the island who could have taken the golden apples. Then – "Yes! I'm sure it's that inlet down there." Rupert cries. "Then let us take a closer look," the griffin growls and Rupert finds he is being borne lower and lower. He is as sure as can be that this inlet is where he saw the vessel ... but where is it now?

The creek is empty, such anxiety,
The real villains have put their boat to sea.

A launch is speeding far, far away –
To catch them now could save the day!

The fleeing launch is very fast,
Griffin's too slow they see at last.

The aircraft, though, is very fast.
Let Rupert go, griffin agrees at last.

"Well?" demands the griffin. "Where is the boat?" "It was here! Just a little while ago when we reached the island!" protests Rupert. By this time they are low enough to see up the wooded inlet. But it's empty all right. Suddenly the harvicopter has swooped and is almost level with them. They turn to see Mr Jack pointing excitedly out to sea. A big powerful launch is racing away from the island and there is a golden glittering in its cockpit. "After it!" roars the griffin.

The fleeing launch is fast. Certainly faster than the griffin, never very swift because of its heavy body, and now lumbered with Rupert. Mr Jack in the harvicopter, which could catch the boat is hanging back to keep an eye on Rupert. "Oh, they'll get away with the golden apples!" pants the griffin. Then Rupert remembers why Mr Jack chose the harvicopter for this trip. "Look, trust us and put me back in the aircraft," he urges the griffin. "We may still save the apples."

Mr Jack must stop the motor
For Rupert to manage to dodge the rotor.

The griffin flies into its place,
Drops Rupert in the cockpit space.

Safe aboard the plane Rupert can
Reveal his rather crafty plan.

Follow the boat, hold the vehicle steady,
Rupert prepares to get everything ready.

"I agree," the griffin pants. At once Rupert signals to Mr Jack that he is going to join him. Mr Jack signals back that he can stop the rotor for only an instant, in which Rupert may be dropped into the cockpit. "I see what to do," says the griffin, as Mr Jack positions the machine both below and in front of it. Mr Jack then holds up his hand. Drops it. The rotor stops. Then, in that single instant, the griffin lunges forward and lets go of Rupert right over the cockpit.

The instant Rupert has dropped safely into the cockpit the griffin swings away and Mr Jack starts the rotor once more. "The griffin can't catch that boat," Rupert tells him. "But we can and 'harvest' the golden apples with the harvicopter." "I guessed that was what you had in mind," replies Mr Jack as he sends the machine surging after the speeding launch. "You work the harvester from the back Rupert." And Rupert who has flown on a harvesting trip before gets everything ready.

RUPERT
harvests the apples

He sets the harvesting machine
To full strength as they reach the scene.

Mr Jack makes the aircraft drop,
To harvest this important crop.

Just as if the fruit was plucked
Into the harvester it's all sucked.

The two men rush despite their fear,
But it's too late; they don't get near.

"Ready?" calls Mr Jack. "Yes, ready!" says Rupert setting the harvicopter's gathering machine to full strength. He looks over the side of the aircraft to find they are almost above the launch. Two men in it are staring, fascinated at the strange aircraft. "Going down!" cries Mr Jack. As the harvicopter drops towards them, the men cower in the shelter of the wheelhouse. "Stand by to harvest!" Mr Jack cries. Rupert moves the lever that lowers the harvicopter's gathering tube.

Rupert leans out of the cockpit to check that the gathering tube is in the right position. Yes. Good. Now he switches on the gathering machine and turns it up to full strength. At this setting the machine would make apple sauce of ordinary fruit, but the heavy golden apples are sucked up undamaged into the body of the harvicopter. The sight of their loot disappearing like this overcomes the men's fear and they scramble desperately towards the golden apples … but just too late.

The plane turns, the two men cower,
Frightened by the griffin's power.

The boat's engine roars into life,
The thieves race off to escape this strife.

The griffin smiles beyond all measure
When he sees the pals' apple treasure!

"Now I must return them to the tree,"
"It only bears fruit once, you see!"

"That's the lot!" calls Rupert as the last of the golden apples is sucked into the harvicopter. At once the aircraft rises and turns back towards the island. The launch doesn't attempt to follow. The two men are cowering, scared, in the wheelhouse, and Rupert sees why. The griffin has caught up and is looming, all ready to swoop on the boat. Before it can, the launch's engine roars and the boat races off at top speed. The griffin turns and follows the harvicopter.

By the time the griffin gets back to the walled garden, the harvicopter has been down for some time and its cargo of golden apples unloaded. "Here you are," Rupert greets it. "Your golden apples are all back." "Thank you," says the griffin. "Forgive me for thinking you took them. Now I must hang them on the tree again for this tree bears fruit but once." "You mean you can't grow more apples from them?" asks Mr Jack. The griffin shakes its head. "Oh dear," says Mr Jack, "How dull."

"Do golden apples have a use?"
The griffin has a poor excuse!

The two pals smile; time to get back,
To the griffin they hand the map.

Mr Jack remembers the way,
No map is needed he does say.

Golden apples hold no allure,
The griffin's happy now, for sure!

"What's the point of golden apples?" asks Mr Jack after examining one. "You can't eat them or anything." "They're for the griffins to guard of course," the griffin replies. That doesn't strike Rupert or Mr Jack as much of an answer, but it's plainly the only one they are going to get, so they smile politely, say they really must be off and climb into the harvicopter. "By the way, you'd better have this," Mr Jack tells the griffin and hands over the chart showing how to get to the island.

As the harvicopter heads homewards Rupert asks Mr Jack, "Without the map how do you know which way to fly?" "I remember the way we came and fly in the opposite direction," Mr Jack says. "I could find my way to the island again. But I shan't. There's nothing there to interest me. Golden apples, huh! Anyway, the griffin will be happier thinking no-one has a map of his silly island."

THE END

RUPERT

and the

Sparklers

John Handd

It's bonfire time and things look good
For the villagers of Nutwood.

But one last item must be found
So Rupert and pals search around.

They comb the wood for leaves and twigs
With sacks to gather all the sprigs.

The pals bring all that they can hold
Save Podgy Pig who alone walks bold.

Nutwood's policeman, PC Growler, has got everyone to agree that this fifth of November they will have just one big bonfire for the village so that he can keep an eye on things. Lots of private ones, he says, can be dangerous. Now the biggest bonfire any Nutwooder can recall is built and Mr Bear perches the Guy on top. All that remains to be done is to get the kindling – brushwood and the like – to set it going and PC Growler gives the job to Rupert and his pals.

Rupert and his pals comb the woods for kindling for the great Nutwood village bonfire. They are careful to take only twigs and branches blown down by the autumn winds, and dry leaves. When they have as much as they can carry they break for the day. But one pal doesn't join them for the walk back to the bonfire. When Podgy Pig emerges from the trees all he is carrying is his sack for dry leaves and it looks far from full. He ignores the pals' calls and scurries off on his own.

Next day where the pals agree to meet
Rupert sees Podgy who fails to greet.

He rushes off in some great hurry
So after him does Rupert scurry.

Why does he sneak off on his own
Through the undergrowth all alone?

Rupert follows the path so sprightly
And spots an object shining brightly.

The pals have agreed to meet the next day to gather more kindling for the great Nutwood bonfire. Rupert is early – but he isn't the first to get to the wood. To his surprise he sees Podgy ahead of him. "Hi!" he calls, "what happened to you yesterday?" Podgy's response is to cast a startled look over his shoulder and scuttle into the trees. Rupert hurries after him and finds a path through the undergrowth but no Podgy. "I'm going to find out what he's up to," decides Rupert.

Rupert starts up the path taken by Podgy, set on finding why his plump chum is acting so oddly. Why does he keep sneaking off on his own? Why is he so keen to avoid his friends? Those thoughts fill Rupert's mind as he follows the path through the thick undergrowth. Then he's brought to a stop. The path forks. Now, which path shall he take? Then he spies something, which makes up his mind for him. On one path, a little way ahead, lies a glittering object, a jewel?

Startled he bends and points a finger
And for a moment dares to linger.

What is that down in the bushes
Through the undergrowth Rupert pushes.

It's like someone has laid a trail
In the darkness his nerves don't fail.

With just the jewel providing light
Rupert is soon in quite a plight.

Surely Podgy can't have dropped the glittering object, thinks Rupert. Why would he have such a thing, anyway? But if he didn't then he can't have taken this path or he'd have seen the thing and picked it up. As Rupert stoops for it his eye is caught by a glow in a sort of low tunnel formed by the bushes. Another of the shining things! He starts into the tunnel to get it. He picks it up and, bless me, if there isn't yet another of them a little way on. All very odd.

"It's as if someone has laid a trail," breathes Rupert at the sight of the third of the glittering things. But so great is his curiosity that even that rather shivery thought doesn't stop him venturing further into the tunnel towards the 'jewel'. It's really dark in this far. As he edges forward the only light is from the 'jewels' he is holding and the one ahead of him. He is almost on it when the earth gives way beneath his feet and he falls into even deeper darkness.

RUPERT
is captured

*He falls into some kind of pit
But how will he climb out of it?*

*A bright light dazzles and then a voice
"Who's that," he cries, he has no choice.*

*Before in protest Rupert can shout,
He's caught in a net, dragged up and out.*

*Lifted up by some unseen hands
He's freed and in the glare he stands.*

The surface Rupert lands on is pretty soft and seems to be covered with some kind of net. He isn't really hurt. It is dark, for the glowing 'jewels' went flying when he fell. But he can make out that he's in a pit. He gets to his feet and starts to explore the sides of the pit to see if he can climb out. He's about to try when he is bathed in dazzling light from above. "Who ... who's that?" he gulps. The voice that answers is stern: "You'll soon see. Now, stand still, sparkler thief!"

Before Rupert can protest that he is not a thief, the earth under his feet seems to come alive. Next moment he finds himself bundled up in a net and hauled out by unseen hands. He sees now that he was right about the 'jewels' being a trail – a trail into a trap! The net is set down and loosened. Rupert picks himself up. For a moment he is too dazzled to make out more than three dim figures behind the light. He rubs his eyes, peers and ..."Them!" he breathes.

"Autumn Elves," he gasps in surprise
With angry expressions Rupert spies.

Three of the little fellows stare
With evil glances at the poor bear.

Blindfolded, with one elf leading
Sounds of silence, there's no pleading.

Up three steps and through a round door
Rupert thinks he's been here before.

"Autumn Elves!" Rupert gasps. Glaring at him are three of a race of little creatures who live under Nutwood. Each autumn they make sure that the mists arrive and the leaves, acorns and the like fall in time. Rupert has several times met the Autumn Elves, including the chief one. Most times they have been friendly enough. This trio plainly is not. Before he can ask what's going on one of the elves snaps: "You're coming with us!" Another blindfolds him and the three march him away.

With one elf holding his arm, Rupert is marched through the wood in a grim silence broken only by the scrunch of dry leaves underfoot. At last the little party halts. Rupert hears what sounds like a door opening. He is led up three steps and helped through what is clearly a doorway. He is edged down steep stairs. He is stopped and his blindfold removed. He blinks and looks around. "I've been here before," he breathes. "You can't have been," an elf scoffs. But Rupert knows he has.

They're taking him to see their chief,
Accused of being a sparkler thief.

A rail car speeds with quiet hum
On winding track until it's done.

"Here he is, caught him red-handed,"
Says one elf once they have landed.

The chief remembers Rupert's help
"Oh please, sir," comes a little yelp.

Despite what his captors care to think, Rupert's adventures have led him to the underground world of the Autumn Elves before. He has even been in the sort of rail car to which he is taken. "You're going to our Chief to let him see what's turned up in our sparkler-thief trap," snaps one elf. Rupert is urged into the rail car, which moves off with a quiet hum and speeds along a winding tunnel. It stops at a pair of large doors. "A prisoner to see the Chief Elf," cries Rupert's escort.

The double doors are thrown open and Rupert is thrust into a brightly lit room. "The sparkler thief!" shouts his escort. "The trail spoiler! Caught red-handed!" Rupert finds himself face-to-face with someone he has met before – the Chief of the Autumn Elves. The Chief stares. "Why, it's Rupert Bear!" he cries. "But I know him. More than once he has even helped us. I cannot believe he is the sparkler thief and trail spoiler!" "Oh, please, sir!" Rupert quavers. "I'm not!"

"I wouldn't steal," our hero pleads
The chief agrees and on he leads.

He takes Rupert out through a door
"Come this way and I'll show you more."

In a room the elves are busy,
He finds out why they're in a tizzy.

The sparklers are to light the trail,
To find their home, they must not fail.

"If I'd known the sparklers were yours I wouldn't have taken them," Rupert pleads. "I thought someone had dropped them. I meant to hand them in to our village bobby." The Chief nods, "I believe you," he says. "Still, you can see why my elves thought you were the sparkler thief." "I suppose so," says Rupert. "But what sparkler thief? And why was I called – what was it – 'the trail spoiler'?" "Come with me and I shall show you," the Chief says, and leads the way to a small door.

At the bottom of some stairs the Chief Elf ushers Rupert into a room marked 'Special Projects'. "This is where we make the sparklers," he explains. "Our backroom boys invented them to help the elves who have been working deep in the woods to find their way back here after darkness falls." Then he leads Rupert to a wall map of the woods and says: "This shows where each sparkler trail leads – or did lead until some wretch yesterday stole a whole lot of them, ruining the trails."

The Chief Elf believes Rupert's tale
But a sudden thought makes Rupert wail.

Podgy was stealing from the wood,
Surely he was up to no good.

About a chum you cannot tell
To the Chief Elf he shall not yell.

Instead he comes up with a plan:
Return the sparklers by noon he can.

"Now, I don't believe that you, Rupert Bear, would take our sparklers and ruin our trails - even if my elves did find you picking up the ones leading to their trap," says the Chief Elf. "I'm so glad you believe me," Rupert cries. "But if you didn't," the Chief continues, "who did?" In that moment Rupert sees in his mind Podgy stealing out of the wood with his sack half full of ... what? "Oh, no!" he groans. "What is it?" hisses the Chief. "You know something, don't you?"

Silence. All eyes are on Rupert. "You know who has our sparklers?" breathes the Chief Elf. "Who?" "Oh, please, I can't say!" begs Rupert. "He's a chum. I can't tell on him. But I'm sure he didn't mean to steal them and that I can get him to return them." Then other elves mutter indignantly but the Chief looks thoughtful. Then he speaks: "I shall give you until noon tomorrow to get our sparklers back because you helped us in the past. But if you don't ..." "Then what?" quavers Rupert.

The angry elf makes plain his threat
To take revenge and make them fret.

A heavy dew will soak each log,
No firework will be seen for fog.

Back to the common Rupert is led
The elf's instructions in his head.

Bring the sparklers back here by noon
Then on this whistle blow a tune.

"If you do not get our sparklers back by noon tomorrow we shall take revenge on everyone in Nutwood," declares the Chief Elf. "The greatest bonfire your village has ever had – oh, yes, we know all about it – will be so soaked in dew, it will never light. What is more, I shall cover the place in such a fog that not a single firework will be seen." "B-but ..." begins Rupert. "No buts!" snaps the Chief. "Just make sure your friend understands. No sparklers – no great Nutwood bonfire!"

Blindfolded and with the Chief Elf's threat ringing in his ears, Rupert is led away. After a while he is guided up steps, a door creaks open and he feels the wind off the common on his face. The blindfold is removed only when he is well away from the exit. The elf with him hands him a little whistle. He speaks: "Tomorrow you will bring the sparklers back to this tree stump and blow the whistle to let us know you are here. From first light we shall be waiting nearby. Now go!"

The sparklers were in Podgy's sack
Rupert thinks as he hurries back.

To Podgy's house he makes his way
Wondering what his friend will say.

On the doorstep he asks outright
If Podgy will return the light.

"No," says Podgy, full of bluster,
With all the cheek that he can muster.

"Those must have been the sparklers in Podgy's sack," Rupert tells himself as he hurries back to Nutwood. "That'll be why he was behaving so oddly." And he decides to waste no time but to call at Podgy's house on his way home. "He can't have known what they were when he found them," Rupert thinks. "Maybe he even meant to hand them in to PC Growler." But remembering how Podgy slunk away, he doubts it. When he reaches Podgy's house he sees him through the window sitting at tea.

"Rupert!" Podgy is surprised to find Rupert on his doorstep so late. "We must talk," Rupert says. "It's very important." "What is?" Podgy asks warily. "That you return at once the sparklers you took from the woods," Rupert says. Podgy's jaw drops. "How do ..." he gasps. Then he recovers: "I don't know what ..." But he sees Rupert isn't going to be taken in, and so he blusters: "Shan't! I found those gem things. I'm sure they're valuable, and finders keepers, so there!"

"You don't understand," Rupert says,
The elves will make sure someone pays.

But Podgy's viewpoint will not budge
The elves, he thinks, could hold their grudge.

Rupert looks so gloomy that night,
Mrs Bear knows something's not right.

He tries to sleep but feels such dread
And worries as he lays in bed.

"You don't understand!" Rupert hisses and he tells of his encounter with the Autumn Elves. "You didn't say I had their things?" Podgy squeaks, alarmed. "No, and I shan't," Rupert says. "But I did say I was sure whoever took them would return them when they knew who they belonged to." "Then you were wrong," grunts Podgy. "Look," Rupert says, "Those sparklers must be given back by noon tomorrow or the Elves will ruin our bonfire!" Podgy only shakes his head and shuts the door.

Glumly Rupert turns away from Podgy's house and makes his way home. He tries to keep his gloom to himself but he has to reassure Mrs Bear that he's all right when she wants to know why he is so quiet. As misery-making as having failed to get back the sparklers, is the thought that Podgy is behaving so badly. Rupert falls asleep telling himself that all that's left now is to throw himself – and the Nutwood bonfire – on the Elves' mercy. But he doesn't think there is really much hope of that.

RUPERT

meets Podgy unexpectedly

Rupert sets out early next day
There's one last chance to get his way.

When Podgy's mother says he's not there
Rupert feels a growing despair.

On his way, in long-faced hush
Finds a surprise behind a bush.

Podgy jumps out, a bag is thrust,
Return the sparklers, that's a must.

Rupert rises early next day. Might as well get it over with – breaking the bad news to the Autumn Elves. He won't tell them who has the sparklers, and sees the Elves won't like that and be even less willing to hear his plea to save the bonfire. As he sets out he decides on a last appeal to Podgy. Podgy's mother comes to the door. "He went out some time ago," she says. "He didn't say where he was off to." As he turns away Rupert sighs, "There goes the last chance."

Gloomily Rupert trudges along towards where he is to meet the Autumn Elves. Then – "Rupert!" He jumps as his name is called and out from behind a bush pops Podgy, plainly embarrassed and carrying a bag that chinks. "I've been waiting for you," he begins. "I just couldn't sleep last night, thinking about the bonfire and how disappointed you'd all be, so ..." He holds up the bag. "Thanks," smiles Rupert reaching for the bag. "No," Podgy says. "I am handing it back and saying sorry."

The pair go boldly to the wood
One whistle signals, things look good.

Two elves appear, ask "Who is this?"
"It's me at fault," Podgy insists.

In the office of the Chief Elf
The bag of sparklers on a shelf.

"What Podgy did was very wrong
To make them takes so very long."

Rupert can see that Podgy is scared as they near the tree stump where he is to meet the Elves. But his plump chum presses on. As arranged, Rupert signals their arrival with the whistle he was given. "Who's this?" demand the two Elves who pop up from a bush. "I'm the one who took your sparklers," quavers Podgy, proffering the bag. "I've come to say sorry." In silence the Elves take the bag, blindfold Podgy, do the same to Rupert with his scarf and march them off into the woods.

The blindfolds are removed only when Rupert and Podgy are in the office of the Chief Elf. The bag of sparklers is on his desk and one of the Elves is whispering to him. Rupert can almost hear Podgy's knees knocking when the Chief fixes a stern gaze on him and speaks: "What you did was wrong, very wrong. Those sparklers take a long time to make. My Elves might have had to spend whole nights in the cold and dark because they could not find their way home thanks to you."

"You brought them back right to our door
About it we shall say no more."

"But never do this thing again
And to all your chums please tell the same."

Now Chief Elf's wrath Podgy has braved
The village bonfire has been saved.

From Willie Mouse there is a shout
"I've found a jewel," he does cry out.

For what seems a long time the Chief Elf says nothing. Then he addresses Podgy: "As I say, you were very wrong to take our sparklers. But not only have you returned them but by doing so yourself have risked our wrath when you needn't have. So we shall say no more about it. But never do such a thing again, and tell all your chums the same. Now go!" So once more Podgy and Rupert are blindfolded and led off. When the blindfolds are removed they are back at the tree stump.

"That was jolly brave of you," Rupert tells Podgy as they hurry down to the village. "The least I could do," Podgy says, although by now he's beginning to feel he has been rather brave. Some of their chums are putting finishing touches to the bonfire when they reach it. Others, it seems, are still off foraging for kindling. One of them is little Willie Mouse. And it's Willie who suddenly rushes down from the woods brandishing something shiny. "I've found a jewel!" he cries.

RUPERT
enjoys the bonfire

The chums grab Willie and swing him round
Straight back to where the jewel was found.

Luckily he remembers where,
Rupert explains about the scare.

PC Growler applies the light,
The bonfire crackles – what a sight.

Old Gaffer Jarge is the true test
"The bonfire this year is the best!"

"What ... where ... why ...?" Willie Mouse gabbles when, without a word, Rupert and Podgy grab him, swing him around and march him back the way he's just come. Quite bewildered, the other pals follow. It is only when a mystified and still startled Willie points out the exact place he found the 'jewel' – luckily he remembers – and puts it back, does Rupert explain what the 'jewel' is, how close they've come to having no bonfire and ends with the Chief Elf's warning.

Bonfire night. All Nutwood is gathered around the great bonfire. When he is sure everyone is well clear, PC Growler puts a flaming torch to the kindling the pals have gathered. As it crackles and roars into life, the crowd gives a mighty cheer. Even Old Gaffer Jarge who seldom admits things are as good as they used to be, cries: "It's the best Nutwood's ever 'ad! Well done, Rupert, you and your chums!"

THE
END

Rupert's Chocolate Patties

*2oz–50g Margarine or Butter
(at room temperature)
2oz–50g Sugar
1 Egg*

*2 Heaped Teaspoons Cocoa
3¹/₂oz–100g Self Raising Flour
Rolled Oats (for coating)*

1. Wash your hands before you begin preparing the food and make sure you have an adult to help you.

2. Have ready a non-stick baking tray, and the oven pre-heated 375°f / gas mark 5.

3. In a mixing bowl, add the butter and sugar and cream together with a wooden spoon until they are combined.

4. Break the egg into a cup lightly whisk with a fork, then add the egg to the butter and sugar mix. Fold in the cocoa and flour and continue to mix with the wooden spoon until all ingredients are thoroughly mixed together; until the mixture has an even dark brown colour.

5. Tip the oats onto a plate, with damp hands shape the mixture into small ball shapes. Roll the balls around in the oats to give a light coating and place onto the baking tray then pat down carefully to flatten slightly.

6. Get the adult helping you to carefully place the baking tray in the centre of the oven. Make sure they are wearing oven-proof gloves.

7. Bake for 15–20 mins, and leave to cool thoroughly before eating.

Remember, do not attempt to cook this recipe without adult supervision.

RUPERT

At Christmas time no trees are there,
The Nutwood folk will have to share.

This Christmas time something awful has happened. Or rather it seemed awful at first. There's a shortage of Christmas trees everywhere. And not one to be had in or near Nutwood! But an answer has been found – right in the middle of the village green. An aged spruce tree that's been there as long as anyone can remember. So why not have one big Christmas tree for the village to share? Everyone, including Rupert and his pals cheers up at once and set about the job of decorating it.

and the Gaffer's guest

An old spruce on the village green –
By all of Nutwood it can be seen.

This Christmas tree will be a sight,
The Professor can power all the light.

Nutwood's answer to the Christmas tree famine – an old spruce growing on the village green as a Christmas tree for all – is going to be a beauty thanks to Rupert's old friend, the Professor. For he has provided the means to light it – a little generator on wheels that he has made. And now on Christmas Eve comes the moment to test it. On come the lights. A great "ooh" of delight rises from everyone ... well, not quite everyone. From behind Rupert comes a grumble: "All right for some!"

On Christmas Eve the lights they test,
Great delight – it will be the best!

RUPERT

listens to Gaffer Jarge

Not everyone shares in the glee,
Gaffer Jarge is grumbling, you see!

Boxes of matches, my, he's in a mire!
Why so many to light his fire?

"Five boxes," repeats Gaffer Jarge,
"I can't afford that kind of charge."

"Each match, a draught just blows it out."
"We'll come to help you," the pals shout.

"Aye, 'tis all right for some folks," the voice repeats. Rupert and his pals turn to see who's grumbling. Standing there is Nutwood's oldest inhabitant, Gaffer Jarge. "Why, what's up Jarge?" asks Rupert. "Don't you like it?" "I suppose it's all right," Gaffer says. "But I've got other things to worry about." "Like what?" the pals want to know. "Well, the price o' matches to start with," Gaffer says. "I've used five boxes since yesterday and I've just been to buy more!"

"Five boxes!" repeats Gaffer Jarge. "That's how many matches I've used up tryin' to light me lamps an' fire, for, as you know, I don't have the electric in me cottage. But every time I strikes a match a draught comes from somewhere I can't find an' blows it out." "Goodness, we can't have that!" cries Rupert. "Look, we'll come home with you, find the draught and block it up." So Rupert, Algy and Bill set off with the old man for his cottage on the edge of the village.

RUPERT

and pals visit Gaffer Jarge

In Gaffer's cottage there is a chill,
The lamp and fire will not light still.

Each time old Gaffer strikes a match,
A wind does blow, the flame won't catch.

Rupert checks the cupboard, a likely source.
But through the air holes he feels no force.

Inside there is a rustling sound.
Opening the door, what has he found?

Gaffer Jarge's cottage, even without 'the electric' is usually cosy with its oil lamps and open fire. But now Rupert and the others shudder at the chilly dimness that greets them. Lamps and fire are ready to be lit. "Watch," says Jarge, and strikes a match near a lamp. At once a puff of draught puts it out. When he strikes another at the fireplace, some way from the lamp, a draught puts it out too. It seems to Rupert that it is coming from the air-holes in a cupboard door.

Rupert advances on the cupboard from which the draught seems to come. There are air-holes in the door to stop the contents getting musty. He holds his hand to them, but there is no trace of a draught. "That's odd," he says and reaches to open the door. As he does so there is a scratchy rustling from inside. He wrenches open the door and gasps at what he sees. Glaring at him and clutching Gaffer's bellows is a prickly twig-like creature. "Raggety!" breathes Rupert. "Oh, not you!"

Rupert explains it is a troll,
Whose home is in a wooded knoll.

Now snow has come and made him hide,
Matches and flames he can't abide.

The troll is selfish and rather bad,
His attitude makes the pals so mad.

"Put it out," the pals hear Algy say,
The troll leaps up, he gets away.

"Wh-what's that?" gasps Gaffer Jarge. "Raggety," Rupert says bleakly. "It's a troll. It lives in or under hollow trees, eating the roots. I first met it when its tree was blown down and I took it home to shelter. It caused no end of bother." "*Now* I'm sheltering *here* because all the tree hollows are full of snow," snaps Raggety, jumping down. "And before you ask, yes, I've been blowing out the matches because, being wood, I hate all flames, as you, Rupert Bear, should well remember!"

Rupert's pals have heard him talk of Raggety but they have never met the troll. Now they see it is every bit as ill-tempered and selfish as he's said. And when they also see that it's ready to have poor old Gaffer go without heat and light, that makes them seethe. "Let's chuck it out!" says Algy. "The three of us can do it." For a moment, Raggety looks as if it will defy the pals, but as Bill and Algy move towards it and Rupert, it gives a wail and leaps for safety.

The troll pleads, "Please don't put me out!"
"I'll freeze outside, there is no doubt."

Then Gaffer Jarge says, "Let it be."
"I will let it stay here with me."

"I'll keep warm in bed," Gaffer says,
"And eat cold food, I have my ways."

The troll speaks up, says he was wrong.
He'll find a new place before too long.

"Oh, please don't put me out!" Raggety bleats. "I'll freeze out there!" "You do have a nerve!" snorts Algy. "You were quite ready to see Gaffer freeze in here!" Even soft-hearted Rupert can't feel sorry for the troll as it shrinks from the pals. "Wait!" It's Gaffer Jarge. "Let it be," he goes on quietly. "We can't put even that out in this weather – especially not this time o'year." The pals stare at the old man who sighs: "I can manage somehow with it in here."

"No, I can't have anyone thrown out o' me home at Christmas," Gaffer Jarge tells Rupert and the others. "I'll go to bed an' keep warm an' I've enough tins o' cold food to keep me going." The pals turn their gaze from Gaffer to Raggety. The troll is silent, its astonished eyes on the old man. Then it gulps and says in a voice quite unlike its usual snap, "No, I'll go. I'll find somewhere. I was wrong to come here." Then it adds as if to itself, "What's come over me?"

Rupert and pals are full of surprise.
"No, he should stay," old Gaffer sighs.

Electric power is the key –
The Professor they dash off to see.

Rupert spells out Gaffer's plight,
What they need for heat and light.

The Professor makes his Christmas appeal;
Will Nutwood's folk the same way feel?

Rupert and his pals goggle at Raggety. "I'm as surprised as you," sighs the troll. "But I mean it. I shall go ..." "No!" breaks in Gaffer. "You wanted to stay here an' stay you shall - 'til Christmas is over anyway." Silence. Then Bills says, "If only Raggety were not scared of flame. If only you had electricity ..." "Wait!" cries Rupert. "I wonder if ... yes, come on, let's see if the Professor is still at the Christmas tree!" Next moment the pals are dashing from the cottage.

Most of Nutwood is still admiring the village's one and only Christmas tree when Rupert and his pals get there. Rupert runs up to the Professor, whose generator is making the electricity for the tree's lights, and speaks to him earnestly. The Professor hears him out, nods, turns to the crowd, holding up his hand for quiet, and addresses them. He tells them of the plight of the Gaffer and Raggety and winds up: "With our generator they could have heat and light ... Well?"

RUPERT
comes to the rescue

Professor's words the good folk heed,
Now, what else will old Gaffer need?

A rush of offers they soon hear ...
Tree lights go out, there is a cheer.

Poor Gaffer can't believe there are
So many things piled in the car!

At last he has both light and heat
And happily he warms his feet.

Are the Nutwooders ready to give up the lights on their only Christmas tree? For that's what it means if the generator goes to the Gaffer and his strange Christmas guest. Rupert holds his breath. Then a voice cries "They are going to need an electric fire. I'll lend that." Then there's a rush of offers – "I'll give a lamp ... a kettle ... an oven ..." The Professor disconnects the generator and as the lights go out there is a cheer louder than the "ooh!" that greeted them.

Gaffer Jarge's jaw drops when he opens his door in answer to Rupert's call. For outside is the Professor's car, piled high with electric lamps, fire, oven and so many other things, and with the generator in tow. Rupert, Bill and Algy unload the car and with Jarge staring pop-eyed and Raggety peeping from the cupboard, put the things in place in the cottage. Then the Professor links them to the little generator, starts it, and in no time light and warmth return to the cottage.

105

As Gaffer and his strange guest wave
The pals recall the joy they gave.

The Christmas tree? Now there's a thing ...
Around it all the villagers sing!

Rupert comes bearing a Christmas treat,
For Gaffer and his guest to eat.

The troll wants some before his lunch,
And picks the holly leaf to munch!

As the Professor, Rupert and the pals drive away from Gaffer's cottage the old man and Raggety stand in the lighted doorway waving goodbye. "Everyone has been splendid," Rupert says. "It's just a pity we shan't have a lighted Christmas tree." But as they near the village green they see a glow and hear the sound of carol singing. Then they round a corner onto the green and there's the whole village, each with a lantern or candle gathered round the tree singing like billy-o.

Christmas morning finds Rupert again at Gaffer Jarge's door. He has brought a present, a Christmas pudding from Mrs Bear. Raggety eyes it hungrily as it's unwrapped. "Can I try a bit now?" He asks. "You're supposed to heat it," protests Rupert. "Don't like it hot," the troll says. "Oh, very well," sighs Rupert. "Lovely!" Raggety cries and, picking a holly leaf off the top, starts to munch it!

THE END

106

1st Prize

'Rupert's Toy Railway' kindly donated by Royal Doulton

It makes up part of a limited edition of only 2,500 copies

2nd Prize

'Rupert's Silver Trumpet' kindly donated by Royal Doulton

For more information on Rupert products by Royal Doulton, please visit: www.royaldoulton.com

3rd Prize

Rupert 1957 Facsimile Collector's Annual

Presented in a protective hard slipcase and with a certificate of authentication, this will be a treasured possession for years to come.

Prizewinners will be notified by post by 31 March 2006 and prizes will be forwarded after this date.

This competition is open to readers of up to and including 10 years of age on 27 January 2006. The competition closing date is 27 January 2006 so all entries must be received by then to be considered. Do make sure the form and the picture do not get detached. Please read the rules on the reverse of this page very carefully to make sure your entry will be accepted.

Enjoy colouring this Rupert picture, then enter the competition. *Fill in your details on the back of this page.*

RULES FOR ENTRY

1. Age and neatness will be taken into consideration in the judging process.

2. You may use pens, pencils, paints or crayons to colour your entry.

3. No entries will be accepted after the closing date.

4. No entries will be accepted without a parent's or guardian's signature to prove the colouring is all your own work.

5. The competition is open to all UK residents aged 10 or under (as of 27 January 2006) other than employees of and relations of employees of Northern & Shell Media, Express Newspapers, the printers and distributors, Royal Doulton and other associated companies.

6. Only one entry per person.

7. There are no cash alternatives to the prizes above.

8. The judges' decision is final; unfortunately no entries can be returned.

9. Express Newspapers reserve the right to use the winning entries for publicity.

10. Express Newspapers cannot accept responsibility for lost, delayed or damaged entries.

11. All entries to be sent to:
    Rupert Bear Colouring Competition 2005,
    Express Newspapers,
    Northern & Shell Building,
    Number 10 Lower Thames Street,
    London EC3R 6EN

ENTRY FORM

Please do not detatch this form from the picture
Please fill in form in block capitals:

NAME _____

ADDRESS _____

_____ POSTCODE _____

TELEPHONE NUMBER _____

E-MAIL ADDRESS _____

AGE AS OF 27 JAN 2006 _____

I certify that this entry is work by entrant only

Signature of Parent or Guardian _____

Please make sure you have read all the rules and are in agreement

Follow Rupert

in the DAILY ✠ EXPRESS and the SUNDAY ✠ EXPRESS

John Harrold

Answers to Puzzles

Spot the Difference

1. Ball 2. Spots changed colour on Mrs Bear's dress 3. Plant pot change of colour 4. Spoon removed from Mr Bear's breakfast bowl 5. Door handle changed colour 6. Top left bauble changed colour 7. Beading removed from door 8. White spots on Mr Bear's tie 9. Chair cushion colour changed 10. Mrs Bear's shoes changed colour

Guess the Story

| Sum Bean | Wind Chimes | Golden Apples | Secret | Sparklers |

| Golden Apples | Sparklers | Secret | Wind Chimes | Speaking Pool | Gaffer's Guest |

| Sum Bean | Wind Chimes | Secret | Speaking Pool | Gaffer's Guest |

The publisher would like to thank the following for their assistance in compiling this book: John Harrold; Gina Hart; Jane Purcell; Royal Doulton; Phil Toze; Sheila Reed.

John Harrold.